FALLING FOR HER BEST FRIEND

A HOLIDAY JUNCTION SWEET ROMANCE

TAMI FRANKLIN

Published by Calava Press

Previously published as *Violet's Valentine.*

Cover images by: stock.adobe.com, © Unique Vision
Cover design by: Tami Franklin

Visit the Author's Web Site at
www.TMFranklin.com

One

Welcome to Holiday Junction, Est. 1898

Violet Chalmers sighed as the bus rumbled past the sign marking her hometown's eastern border. They'd already switched the decorations—wide pink and red ribbons wrapped around the two side support posts, and the plaque featuring clinking New Year's champagne glasses had been replaced with a big red heart. Valentine's Day was coming, and as usual, Holiday Junction was ready.

Vi should have felt warm and cozy about coming home, but instead, the failure that sat in her stomach like a rock rolled around a bit, and she swallowed against a wave of nausea. Ben would have mocked her for that, called her melodramatic and overemotional. He—

No. She wasn't going to think about Ben. Not right now.

Instead, Vi dug in her purse for a compact and lip gloss, grateful that there was no one in the seat beside her. If there was one thing Vi couldn't have handled on the long trip from New York, it was making conversation with a stranger. She frowned at her reflection and patted on some powder in a fruitless attempt to hide the dark circles under her eyes. They were expected after a six-and-a-half-hour flight and a three-and-a-half-hour bus ride, but no less jarring. Her mother was sure to notice them . . . and just as sure to comment on them. She swiped on a little pink gloss and shrugged. This was as good as it was going to get.

Vi tucked away her things as the bus splashed through the slushy puddles and pulled up to the Greyhound station at the edge of town. Dirty, gray snow still sat in piles around the low, dingy concrete building, but most of it had melted on the sidewalk and parking lot. Holiday Junction was in that murky drabness between the sparkling snow-covered brilliance of winter and the pink-budded beauty of spring. The bus hissed to a stop and Vi stood, drawing her bag over her shoulder and bracing herself for what was coming.

She didn't want to be there. But she didn't really have a choice.

Following the line of bedraggled travelers down the aisle, she spotted her mother waving wildly from beside her little red car. Despite herself, Vi couldn't keep from smiling. Louise Chalmers—Lou to her friends—was a force of nature with her spiky blonde hair, a few shades lighter than Vi's own, Audrey Hepburn sunglasses, and a black wool coat over jeans and wedge-heeled leather boots. Her mom would be fifty-two on her next birthday but didn't look a day over forty. Thanks, she was quick to say, to her hairdresser, monthly facials, and a glass of red wine with dinner every night.

She hurried over to the bus just as Vi stepped off. "You're here!" she said, pulling her daughter into a tight hug. "It's about time!"

"Hi, Mom." Why was it no matter how old you were, a hug from your mom made you feel like you were ten years old?

"Are you hungry? You must be hungry. I have some cookies in the car." She pulled back, holding on to Vi's shoulders as she scrutinized her face. "You look tired. Are you sure you're all right?"

Vi resisted the urge to roll her eyes—barely. "I'm fine. Just a long trip."

Lou frowned, not buying it. "It's Ben, isn't it? You don't need him, honey. He doesn't deserve—"

"It's not Ben," she said, maybe a little too loudly. Vi cleared her throat and lowered her voice. "I promise. I'm fine. I just need some sleep and maybe dinner?"

"Of course!" Vi waved a hand. "You must be starving. I can't believe you wouldn't let me pick you up in Seattle. We could have gotten a nice dinner at that seafood place—"

"I wasn't going to make you drive all the way to Seattle," Vi replied quickly. "Besides, I like the drive. It was nice to see the mountains." That part was true. The Cascades were beautiful at this time of year and it was one thing she had missed while she was in New York.

They retrieved Violet's bags and packed them into the car, smooshed between the boxes and bins from her mother's various events. Lou was on the planning committee for all of the town's festivities—and when you lived in Holiday Junction, there were a *lot* of town festivities. As the brochure said, *Holiday Junction is the place to celebrate every holiday . . . and it's where the holidays come to celebrate.*

No, it didn't really make sense, but it got the point across.

"How was your flight?" Lou asked once they'd gotten into the car and pulled out of the parking lot. "Did they give you anything to eat besides mustard pretzels?" She made a face.

Vi laughed. “I had a sandwich,” she said. “But I've been dreaming about your roasted chicken . . .” She gave her mom a hopeful look.

“Well, you're in luck,” Lou said, turning onto Main Street. “It's in the oven and should be about ready once we get home.” She smiled and patted her daughter's leg.

“Can't wait,” she replied, looking out the window. “The town looks good. The same.”

And it did. Holiday Junction seemed to be trapped in time—a quaint small town that looked like it had been plucked out of somewhere in New England and plopped down into a mountain valley in central Washington. Store fronts bore striped awnings and stately columns, wood and brick facades and brightly painted doors. And, of course, the holiday decorating was already underway.

“They have the lights changed,” Lou said, pointing up at the pink and red twinkle lights twined through the trees running down both sides of the street. “But the mayor thinks we need new hearts for the lamp posts and it's causing a whole thing—” She twirled her fingers in the air. “So that pushed everything back and now we're behind schedule.”

“Well, it's not even February yet,” Vi pointed out.

“It will be tomorrow.” Lou pushed her sunglasses

up and shot her an offended look. "Besides, there's a schedule for a reason," she said. "Holiday Junction isn't Holiday Junction—"

"—without the holidays," Vi finished with her.

She pursed her lips. "It's just another—"

"—small town that's nothing special."

"I hate it when you do that." Lou turned the corner, but her lips quirked.

"Sorry," Vi said. "You're right. The mayor is being unreasonable, and the schedule must be kept!" She pounded a fist on the armrest.

"Do you want me to turn this car around?" Lou flicked on her blinker. "Because I will turn this car around."

"No!" Vi folded her hands, begging. "Mom, if you do, who will eat the roasted chicken? Think of the chicken!"

Lou fought it for a moment, then burst out laughing. "I'm so glad you're home."

Well, Violet couldn't say exactly that, so she settled for, "Love you, Mom."

They pulled into the driveway in front of Violet's childhood home, a bungalow with a wide front porch and white shutters. "You painted the house," she said. The main floor was no longer green, but a pale blue, the second-story dormer a darker blue, and the front door, bright yellow.

"Didn't I tell you that?" Lou asked as she put the car in park. "I think it's better, don't you? Cheerful."

"Yeah, it's nice," Vi replied, getting out of the car. Her eyes drifted to the similar house next door, painted in shades of gray with white trim. "Hey, is Kade still around?"

"Hmm? Oh, yes. Such a nice kid. He helped me out when the furnace broke last month." She opened the trunk and yanked out one of Vi's suitcases. "I better check the chicken," she said, rolling it toward the front steps. "Can you get the rest?"

"Sure, no problem." Violet rounded the car, her gaze taking in the street where she played as a child; learned to drive as a teenager. Like most things around Holiday Junction, it hadn't changed much. The trees were a little taller, maybe, and the historic street lights now had LED bulbs, but other than that it looked pretty much the same.

Ten years. It had been just shy of ten years since she'd been back. Vi felt bad about that, but as a struggling actress, she could never afford the trip. Money was tight for her mom, as well, but she'd made it to New York a few times over the years—twice for Christmas, the two of them crammed in Vi's tiny apartment. It had been fun to share the city with her mom during the holidays. They'd walked through Central Park, ice skated in front of Rockefeller Center, and ooh-ed and ahh-ed over the extravagant window displays.

Of course, the last time Lou had flown out, it was after everything had happened—after Ben had left, and—

Well, it was not a fun trip, that one.

Vi sighed, her stomach rumbling. It was only a little after four, but she'd been up since three in the morning, New York time, and hadn't had much to eat other than the sandwich on the plane. She tugged on her bigger suitcase, frowning when it refused to budge.

"Come on," she muttered, shoving aside one of her mom's boxes before taking hold of the bag once again. "Come on, I've got chicken waiting." She propped a foot up on the bumper and pulled harder. It barely moved, so she took a deep breath, tightened her grip, and gave it a good hard jerk.

The bag came flying out and knocked her back. Vi fought to maintain her balance, but failed, landing on her backside with a grunt. The suitcase hit the concrete driveway and the zipper gave, the bag bursting open in a shower of clothing and accessories.

"Perfect," Vi muttered.

"Need some help?" a voice asked.

She startled, looking up to find a man watching her with humor in his eyes, and various items of silky clothing draped over his extremities. Vi scrambled to her feet, vainly attempting to brush the dampness off the back of her jeans. "I am *so* sorry," she said, grabbing the clothing and wadding it up under her arm. She froze, finally focusing on the guy.

"Kade?"

He winked. "Hey, Vi. Heard you were back in town."

She tossed the ball of clothes into the trunk and threw her arms around his neck. "It's so good to see you!" she mumbled into his skin. He smelled really nice.

Kade hesitated for a moment, then returned the hug. "Good to see you, too."

They pulled apart, and she was surprised to find herself looking up a little more than she used to. "Did you get taller?"

He laughed, brown eyes crinkling at the corners. "Since high school? Yeah, maybe a little."

Kade was definitely taller . . . and bigger. Well,

he was still lean, but not skinny like in high school. His shoulders were broader, too. Dark hair cropped short, and was that—

She reached out before she could think better of it and scratched at the stubble covering his cheek. "This is new, too."

He swiped at her hand. "Give me a break. I didn't have time to shave today!"

Vi's mouth dropped open and she pressed a palm to her chest in mock surprise. "You're *shaving* now?"

"Shut up."

"*You* shut up!"

"That's it." He grabbed her around the neck and began to rub his knuckles on her head. "Say it!"

"No!" she shrieked, struggling against his grip.

"Say it!"

"Let me go!" She couldn't keep from laughing.

"Not until you say it!"

Vi collapsed against him, defeated. "Kade is the king," she mumbled.

"And . . ." he prompted.

She let out an annoyed sigh but was still giggling. "And I am but his lowly servant. Now let go!"

He released her immediately, a smug smile on his face. "Glad we're in agreement."

"I take it back. You haven't changed a bit." She grinned at him. "You're as annoying as ever."

His eyes widened. "I resemble that remark."

She groaned. "You're *still* saying that?"

"Only to you," he replied, and the thought made her feel warm all over. She'd missed him. He had been her best friend and they'd drifted apart over the years, but somehow, it seemed like no time had passed at all.

She smiled. "So, how have you been?"

He shrugged. "Good. You know, the usual. Filling young minds with the wonders of Calculus."

"Ugh." Vi grimaced. "I can't believe you enjoy teaching *math.* I could barely tolerate it when I had to take it."

"It's a dirty job, but somebody has to do it." He slid his hands into his jacket pockets and kicked one booted foot against the driveway. "I hear you'll be joining our distinguished faculty at good old HJHS."

She extended her arms with a flourish and gave a little bow. "The new choir and drama teacher, at your service. I start on Monday."

He winced. "I assume you know the reason for the sudden job opening."

"I might have heard something about the former

teacher, a bottle of moonshine, and a rather unfortunate incident of streaking?"

Kade shook his head. "Bertram Russell naked in the town square. That's something you can never unsee."

"Sounds traumatic." She shuddered. "Well, fortunately, I have my lesson plans all ready to go, and auditions for the spring musical are already done, but any survival tips would be much appreciated."

"Well, avoid the coffee and the vending machines and you should be fine," he said. "And the moonshine, of course."

"Of course." Vi nodded sagely.

Kade looked down at his feet for a moment. "I saw you on TV. In that commercial for the orange juice?"

"Oh no!" She covered her face. They'd made her wear a goopy facial mask for that one.

"No, you were good!" Kade pulled her hands down. "You were always really good."

And that—that was something she really didn't want to talk about. "Well, at least one person thought so." Before he could say anything more, she added. "You want to join us for dinner? Mom's making roasted chicken."

She held her breath, hoping he'd drop the subject. He did, of course. Kade had always understood her.

"I wish I could," he said. "But I have to be somewhere—" He looked at his watch. "—right now." He backed away toward his car, a black SUV. "Rain check?" he asked.

"Sure," she replied. "We need to catch up."

He nodded and got in his car and drove away, leaving Vi surrounded by a broken suitcase and piles of dirty, wet clothing.

"Good to be home," she mumbled as she gathered it all up and headed inside. At least there'd be a hot bath and a good meal waiting.

It took a good ten minutes before Kade's heartbeat returned to normal. He'd heard Violet was coming home—he did live next door to her mom, after all—but seeing her when he wasn't prepared . . .

Well, it caught him off guard. That's all it was. He was surprised to see her in the driveway, then her suitcase exploded, and she teased him like when they were kids and—

Yeah, it made perfect sense that his palms would

get sweaty and his heart would race and his skin would get all tingly.

A completely reasonable reaction.

He turned the corner, heading for the Baxter house on the other side of town. Sam Baxter was one of his guitar students—teaching math didn't exactly have him rolling in dough, so he taught music on the side. Kade enjoyed sharing his love for music with kids who were a little more enthusiastic than his math students.

Why did everyone hate math so much? It was so *cool*!

Kade inhaled deeply and caught a whiff of Vi's perfume where it clung to his jacket. She smelled different than he remembered. Not that he spent a lot of time smelling her back in high school.

Not that he hadn't *wanted* to.

But back then, Vi was part of Vi-and-Liam, the golden couple of Holiday Junction High School. And Kade was Vi's best friend.

Which wasn't *bad*, don't get him wrong. Violet Chalmers was an awesome friend, and they'd been inseparable since, well, pretty much since birth. They'd grown up next to each other and their mothers had been close friends.

But somewhere around sophomore year, Kade had turned to look at Vi and she'd smiled and he—

Well, things had changed. He wasn't sure if he fell in love with Vi in that moment, or if he'd been in love with her all along, and just then realized it.

Not that it mattered.

Vi-and-Liam, remember?

Kade sighed and pulled into the Baxter's driveway. They were old friends of the family, but then again, having lived in HJ all his life, *most* people were friends of the family. He parked, pulled his guitar case out of the back seat, and walked up to the front door. It opened before he knocked and a young girl with long blonde hair gave him a rather imperious look before stalking past him toward the sidewalk.

Sam Baxter stood behind her, looking rather forlorn. "Hi, Mr. Rivera," he said glumly. "Come on in."

He followed the boy into the living room, waving at his mother, Lisa, in the kitchen before he shrugged off his coat.

"Everything okay, buddy?" he asked as he sat down on the couch and pulled out his guitar.

Sam shrugged, tuning his own instrument. "Girl trouble."

Kade blinked. "Aren't you a little young for that?" he asked without thinking.

Sam's blue eyes narrowed. "I'm eleven."

"Sorry." He held up his hands, defensively. "You want to talk about it?"

He shrugged again. "She said she wanted to watch my lesson. But then Jamie Daughtry texted her and she decided she'd rather go hang out with him."

"Ah." Kade felt for him. The kid looked crushed. "That's too bad, man."

"I just don't understand women," Sam said, his guitar balanced precariously on his lap. "How are we supposed to know what they want?"

"Preaching to the choir," Kade said sympathetically. "But if she can't see how awesome you are, it's her loss, you know?"

For some reason, Kade's thoughts drifted to Violet again. It was good to see her. Like old times. It would be nice to have her around without the specter of Kade's unrequited love hanging over their heads. They could be friends again, like they used to be.

That would be nice. Great. It would be great. Right?

"Mr. Rivera?"

He smiled. "Sorry, what?"

"I said, do you think if I learned to play really good—"

"Well—"

Sam didn't miss a beat. "—really *well* that I could be in a band? I mean, girls love rock stars, right?"

"You're not going to be in a band!" his mom yelled from the kitchen. "Not until you graduate!"

Sam rolled his eyes and Kade tried not to laugh, leaning in conspiratorially. "I've heard that, yes," he whispered.

The boy grinned and picked up his guitar. "What's first? Dylan or the Beatles?"

Kade positioned his own guitar. "You pick."

They strummed out *Eleanor Rigby,* and Kade put all thoughts of Violet Chalmers aside, for now.

Two

The next evening, Kade stood at Vi's door, wondering if he should knock or ring the doorbell. Over the past few years, he hadn't bothered with either, at Lou's insistence. He'd just call out as he entered so she knew he was there.

But things were different now. And he felt weird simply barging in.

He felt weird about a lot of things, actually.

Like when Vi had showed up at *his* doorstep earlier in the day to invite him for dinner.

"Mom's making meatloaf," she'd cajoled, as if he'd needed any cajoling. Lou's meatloaf was his favorite.

He played it cool, though. "I don't know," he said, tapping his lips thoughtfully. "We had meatloaf last week."

She looked affronted. "You've been eating my mom's meatloaf without me?"

"You weren't here!"

"That's no excuse!" She pointed at him, then

jabbed the finger into his chest to accentuate her words. "You should have abstained in my memory."

"From meatloaf," he said flatly.

"Absolutely!" She poked him again. "For the sake of our friendship."

"Stop poking me." He grabbed her finger. "And what did you expect? For me to pine away over that meatloaf for years? I'm a man with needs, Vi."

She snorted. "Typical."

"And would you rather have some stranger enjoying your mom's meatloaf?" he asked, jiggling her finger. "At least you know I truly appreciate it."

Vi laughed. "Well, are you going to appreciate it tonight or not?" she asked. "Because, if not, I can ask someone else—" She backed up a step.

"Don't you dare," Kade replied, yanking her back by the finger. "I'll be there."

And as she bumped up against him, he caught another whiff of her perfume—something vanilla-y and floral, maybe? Was that a thing? Vanilla flowers?

Anyway, he suddenly realized how close they were standing and dropped her finger like a hot potato, his face heating. He rubbed the back of his neck. "So, what time's dinner?"

Vi gave him a funny look but didn't say anything

about his strange behavior. "Six-ish? Come by anytime so we can catch up."

She'd left then, saying she had to get some prep work done for class the next morning. And for some unknown reason, Kade had changed his shirt three times before heading next door at six.

He settled on knocking, and Vi opened the door a few moments later. "Hey. Come on in." She eyed his neatly pressed shirt. "You look nice."

Kade felt his face heat. "Thanks. So do you." She was wearing leggings and a flowy floral top that draped off her shoulders.

"Oh, this old thing?" She grinned at him and took his coat.

He followed her into a kitchen he knew as well as his own. White cabinets with glass inserts showed off Lou's collection of brightly colored dishes. She'd put in new countertops a few summers ago—gray quartz—with a farmhouse sink and a butcher block island in the middle of the room.

Lou stood at the stove, stirring gravy and waved them toward the breakfast nook. "Set the table, would you?" she asked no one in particular.

Kade took up the task and retrieved plates while Vi grabbed the silverware. They worked in tandem, like they had so many times in the past, and once again Kade was struck by how easily they'd fallen back into their old relationship.

They'd been so close, back then. And when Vi had left, they'd both promised that nothing would change. It did, of course. They were kids, after all, and living different lives. The calls and emails became more infrequent until they trailed off altogether, and eventually they had moved on. Lou had filled him in on what Vi was up to, and he assumed she did the same for Vi, but other than that? Well, Kade had assumed their friendship was over. That it had died a quiet death, starved by neglect.

Which made it all the more remarkable that as soon as they saw each other again, it was like no time had passed at all. They'd picked up right where they left off—teasing and joking and laughing together.

"You put the fork on the wrong side," Vi said with a glint in her eye. This was a familiar debate.

"It's on the *right*, Chalmers," he said, "so how can it be wrong?"

She rolled her eyes. "Everyone knows the fork goes on the left, you Philistine. It's proper etiquette."

"Etiquette, schmetiquette." Kade waved a hand. "We're all right-handed. Why should we reach *all* the way across the plate to grab our fork?" He demonstrated, overemphasizing the long stretch as he wiggled his fingers over the knife he placed on the left. "It's more efficient this way."

"Lazy, you mean." Vi sniffed.

"Children!" Lou said sharply. "Sit down. It's time to eat."

Kade grinned at Vi, and she stuck her tongue out at him before smiling herself. He sat in his usual place, across from the window looking out over the back yard. The cherry tree was just showing hints of budding.

"You need to get that sprayed this year," he said.

Lou brought over the bowl of mashed potatoes and sat down, flicking out her napkin before laying it across her lap. "I know. I've already set it up."

He nodded. "You want me to prune it?"

She eyed the tree thoughtfully. "Maybe a little. Gotta do it before the buds break."

"I can come by this week after school sometime when the weather's nice. I'll take care of that broken bit of fence, too." He felt a little prickle on the back of his neck and turned to see Vi watching him. "What?" he asked.

She blushed, but only shook her head. "Nothing." Vi handed him the platter of meatloaf.

He took a few slices and searched for something to say, suddenly feeling tension in the room.

"So, are you all ready for Monday?" he finally asked.

Violet swallowed and took a sip of her water. "I think so. I'm a little nervous, though. It's weird to come in mid-year."

"You'll be great," Lou said, pouring gravy on her potatoes. "Those kids are lucky to have you. A real Broadway star!"

"Mom—" Vi looked decidedly uncomfortable. "I'm no star. I had a few small parts, is all. And it wasn't even Broadway. It was off-off-*way off*-Broadway."

"Doesn't matter," Lou said stubbornly. "You have real life experience."

"That's one thing to call it," she muttered.

"Don't sell yourself short," Kade said, pointing at her with his fork. "You are extremely talented. Always have been."

"Tell that to the casting directors." She stabbed at her broccoli.

"Hey." He grabbed her hand. "I don't know a lot about the business, but I do know that it's tough. And that talent doesn't always equate success."

"So what does failure equate?" she asked.

"You're not a failure." Kade squeezed her hand before returning to his meal. "And stop feeling sorry for yourself. It's extremely unattractive." He shot her a mischievous look and her lips twitched.

"*You're* extremely unattractive," she grumped, but the mood had lifted, so Kade felt like he'd done his job.

"So, fill me in on the last decade," Vi said later as they sat on the porch swing, sipping cocoa. She waggled her eyebrows at Kade, "Romance-wise."

Dinner had been fun, just like she remembered, with Kade's sharp wit clashing with her own snarky comments, and Lou throwing up her hands in irritation at them both. It had been like old times, and Vi was equal parts amazed at how they still clicked, and saddened that she'd let them drift apart for so long.

Lou had eventually left them to their cocoa and headed to her craft room to work on some Valentine decorations for the shop. Lou took the competition between local business owners very seriously when it came to decorating. And *Chalmers' Chapters*, the local used bookstore that had been in her family for three generations, always had an impressive display. It had been tough when Vi's dad died fifteen years earlier of a heart attack, and Lou had almost sold the shop, unable to walk through the doors without seeing the ghost of Ed Chalmers. But in the end, practicality won over—she had a daughter to raise and bills to pay, after all—and in time, Lou had come to love running *Chapters* on her own.

Vi was glad. She couldn't imagine walking into the store and not seeing her mom behind the counter.

"Romance-wise?" Kade sipped his cocoa and rolled his eyes. "Not much to tell," he said. "Few dates here and there—"

"Ooooohhh . . ." Vi said, teasing.

"No *oooohhh* about it," he said. "Nothing serious. No one special." He shrugged. "How about you?"

Vi's stomach twisted into knots. "Well, there was this guy . . ."

"Ben."

"You know about Ben?"

"Lou told me."

Of course. *Perfect.* "What exactly did she tell you?" Vi was going to kill her mother.

"Not much, really," he replied. "Just that you were dating him. He's an actor, too. That's about it."

The fact he wouldn't meet her eyes made her think it was a bit more than that.

"Ben was—" Vi sighed, trying to think of the

right words. "—a mistake. I think. I don't know. It seemed so perfect. He was a lot of fun. Very spontaneous. Kind of sassy—like you a little bit, now that I think of it."

He gave her a look of distaste. "I am *not* sassy," he retorted. "*Cats* are sassy!"

She laughed. "Sarcastic, then. Snarky. Irreverent . . . whatever." She swallowed some of her chocolate, which had gone lukewarm. "Anyway, long story short, I thought we had a lot in common. He said he loved me. We even talked about marriage, someday. But then about six months ago, he got a big part in a Broadway show and unceremoniously dumped me for his leading lady. And that was that."

Vi hoped saying it like that—quick and unemotional—would hide how much it devastated her.

Apparently, it didn't, because Kade said, "I'm so sorry. What a jerk."

"Yeah." She gulped down the rest of her cocoa. "I got fired from my waitressing job for calling in sick for an audition—I didn't get the part, big surprise—and I couldn't make rent, so . . ." She felt so pathetic, but it was nice to finally tell someone all of it. Well, most of it, anyway. Only her mom knew it all, and Vi planned to keep it that way.

She sipped her cocoa. "I called Mom and told

her I was coming for a visit. Then I found out about the job at the school and I figured, what the heck, right? I can work for a while, build up a nest egg, and I'll be able to try again in a year or so." She looked out over the front yard to the shadowy street beyond. "Maybe L.A. this time. Who knows?"

"L.A.," Kade said flatly. "Right."

She looked at him. "What's wrong?"

He opened his mouth to say something, but hesitated, snapping it shut before shaking his head. "I was just getting used to having your around again, you know?" he said finally. "And you're already talking about leaving."

"Well, I'll be around for a while," she said nudging his shoulder with her own. "The rest of this school year, and probably next year, too. You'll get sick of me."

Kade's lips quirked before he took another drink of his cocoa. "Too late."

She gaped at him and smacked him on the arm. "You are such a jerk!" Then she noticed a smear of whipped cream on the stubble above his lip. "You have a little something." She motioned toward her own face.

He stuck out his tongue, swiping the left side of his mouth, then the right. "Did I get it?"

Vi wrinkled her nose. "No, it's right—" She pointed at his upper lip, right below his nose. His tongue darted out but was nowhere near long enough to reach it.

"Just . . . hold still," she said, laughing, reaching out to wipe the smear off with her thumb. Her fingers drifted across his cheek, and she was surprised to find his beard soft, instead of prickly. Her gaze locked with his for a moment, his brown eyes warm and teasing. Vi felt suddenly self-conscious and pulled away, wiping her thumb on her jeans as she swallowed nervously.

"Is it gone?" he asked quietly, his voice husky.

She didn't look at him. "Yeah, I got it."

They sat in silence for a moment, the air heavy around them as the swing creaked rhythmically. She should probably head in and go to bed, but she couldn't quite bring herself to do so, and Kade gave no sign he was ready to leave.

"Have you seen anyone else since you've been back?" he asked after a while.

"Hmm?" Vi glanced at him. "Like who?"

He shrugged. "I don't know. Anyone from school? Liam, maybe?" He shot her a sideways glance.

"Liam?" She let out a huff of surprise. "I haven't thought of Liam in—Is he still in town?" she asked.

Kade looked away, out over the yard. "Sure. He's a lawyer now. Has his own practice." His foot pushed the swing a little faster. "I'm surprised you didn't know."

"Well, we haven't really kept in touch." Her thoughts drifted to sandy hair, blue eyes, and moonlit nights out at the Point. "It would be nice to see him again," she said. "If he's not still mad at me."

Kade snorted. "It's been ten years. I think he's probably over you dumping him."

"I didn't *dump him*," Vi said, smacking his leg. "I *broke up* with him because we were going to college on different sides of the country and I didn't think we were ready for a long distance relationship."

"Potato. Po-tah-toe," Kade replied, handing her his mug. "I should go. We both have an early day tomorrow."

"Ugh. Monday. Don't remind me," Vi said, standing as he did. "I guess I'll see you at school?"

He glanced toward the driveway. "Do you need a lift?" he asked. "We don't have Uber around here, so . . ."

"Well, I was going to walk, but if you're offering, that would be great."

"I'm offering," he said, heading down the steps. "I leave at seven. Don't be late."

"Seven?" She groaned. "Man, I miss being an out-of-work actor. It has much better hours."

Vi heard him laugh as he walked home in the darkness. "See you tomorrow," he called out as he climbed his own front porch.

"Good night," she replied, settling down on the swing again. She wasn't tired, wasn't used to going to bed so early. Setting the mugs down on the porch, she started the swing rocking again with her toe.

Liam Durant. Now that was a name she hadn't thought about in years. She had been crazy about him in high school—they'd been crazy about each other—and the two of them had been nearly insepa-rable for almost three years. Liam had been the golden boy of Holiday Junction High School—foot-ball captain, student body president, honor student—and he'd been just about the handsomest guy she'd ever seen. She'd had a terrible, all-encompassing crush on him—one that Kade had heard about endlessly, God bless him—and she'd wished and prayed that one day he'd notice her.

Then one day, he did. He approached her at her locker with that dazzling smile and those blue, blue eyes, and asked her to the Homecoming dance sophomore year. They'd been together ever since.

But Violet never planned on staying in Holiday Junction . . . and once she left, she'd never planned on coming back. She was going to go to New York to become a Broadway star. It was her dream, and she knew, even at eighteen, that Liam wasn't going to be a part of it.

So, they'd had that wonderful summer after graduation. And the weekend before he headed to UCLA and she headed to Connecticut, she'd ended it. He'd been hurt, of course, and surprised—although at the time, Vi couldn't understand why. She'd thought she was being practical. Logical. High school was over and they had different plans for their lives, so why try to drag something out that was destined to end eventually?

Since then, she'd had moments when she'd regretted the decision. At least how she handled it, if not what she'd actually done. It had been cold, she knew. Not very nice.

But the past was the past, Vi thought with a sigh. And here she was right back where she started.

Liam Durant.

She whispered the name out loud, just to see how it felt.

It felt nice.

Maybe coming back to Holiday Junction wasn't such a bad thing after all. She had her friend back, which was awesome. And it would be fun to see Liam again. Just to talk . . . catch up, nothing more.

She leaned back in the swing and gazed up at the stars, lost in thoughts and memories.

Three

Vi was standing by Kade's car when he left the house the next morning. Bundled up with a red knitted scarf wound around her neck and a stocking cap perched on her blonde head, she looked like a ski bunny ready to hit the slopes. She held a steaming travel mug of coffee with both hands, sipping at it gingerly.

"I forgot how cold it is at seven in the morning in February," she said as he approached.

Kade shook his head with a mocking smile. "The Big Apple made you soft, Chalmers." He unlocked the car and tossed his satchel into the back seat.

"We have *subways*, Kade," she said longingly. "Subways are warm."

He grimaced. "And they smell like B.O. and pee."

She shrugged. "A minor drawback."

They got in the car, and Kade blasted the heat as he backed out of the driveway. Violet let out a little moan of appreciation when the air finally warmed and held her hands up to the vent. “So what can you tell me about the principal, Ms. Beatty?” she asked.

He blinked at her in surprise. “You haven't met her?”

“Only over the phone and Skype,” she replied. “I wasn't able to fly out for an interview, so we did it online. She seemed nice enough. Supportive.”

He smirked. “Desperate.”

“Hey!” She hit his arm, barely avoiding spilling her coffee. “But yeah, you're probably right. It must be tough to lose a teacher mid-year.”

They talked a bit about the school and the staff until they pulled into the faculty parking lot at Holiday Junction High School. The school hadn't changed much since they graduated, Kade thought, trying to see it through Violet's eyes. Lots of red brick and concrete—a grassy courtyard at the center of four wings arranged like spokes around a wheel.

“Bring back fond memories?” he asked as they approached the entrance.

Vi smiled. “Go Bearcats!” She threw up a fist, and Kade laughed.

She followed Kade into the office, which actually had changed a bit. The drab gray carpet had been replaced by more drab gray carpet, and the fluorescent lights replaced by LEDs.

HJHS was nothing if not energy conscious.

Kade probably could have left Vi there and headed to his own room to prepare for the day. But he felt somewhat responsible for her—it being her first day and all—so he hung out while the secretary, Lydia, gave her room keys, a school map (like she needed one of *those*), and a binder containing school policies, emergency procedures, phone numbers, and the like.

"You're supposed to review it all before you start," Lydia told her. "But given this is an unusual situation, we're forgoing protocol just a bit." She waited a beat, and Kade knew she was waiting for Vi to ask about the *unusual situation*. Lydia tended to be a bit of a gossip.

"Okay, then, I'll show you to your room," Kade said, grabbing Vi's elbow and steering her out of the office. "See you later, Lydia!"

The secretary waved, disappointment evident on her features, and he released Vi once they were out of sight. "Sorry," he said. "You would have been there for twenty minutes if she got started."

"Thanks," Vi said, offhanded. She was looking around the hallway, examining the signs on the walls as they walked. "It's so weird," she said. "It's different, but it's exactly the same, if that makes sense."

"Well, wait until the kids get here and you'll see how different it is," he replied. "We have about a third more student body now than we did back then . . . all crammed into the same sized building."

"Great." She came to a stop at the double doors to the Commons–the center of the school, where all the hallways converged. It was empty at this time of day, tables and chairs lined up against the walls for use at lunchtime. Vi walked in and turned a slow circle, her eyes drifting to the skylights overhead.

"Remember the Homecoming dance, sophomore year?" she asked.

"I've been to a dozen Homecoming dances," he replied. For some reason, he really didn't want to talk about that particular dance. "It's hard to remember them all."

"Going as a chaperone doesn't count." She shook her head. "It was so much fun. They hung little twinkle lights all up there." Vi waved toward the ceiling. "It was a Great Gatsby theme, and they had all those gold and black balloons, and a champagne fountain–"

"–it was Sprite."

She arched a brow. "So you *do* remember."

"Hard to forget a Sprite fountain." He made a

face. "And all those feathers. I was picking them out of places for weeks."

"Now *that* I didn't need to know," she said, cringing. "Way to taint the memory of a magical night."

"Magical? Seriously?"

"It was! I wore this sparkly dress and Liam kissed me for the first time right over there." Vi tilted her head toward the corner. "Who did you go with? I can't remember. Was it Amy?"

"Amy? No." He laughed, shaking his head. "No, I believe for that illustrious event, I went stag."

"That's right!" She pointed at him, and he got a sinking feeling. "We did the dance that night. Do you remember?"

"Nope," he said quickly. "I have absolutely no recollection of any such thing."

"Oh, yes you do." Vi began to bounce from foot to foot, rhythmically, reaching for his hands.

He pulled them back quickly. "I do not!"

But he totally did. For some unknown reason, Vi had been obsessed with swing dancing the summer after ninth grade. And for some unknown reason, Kade had gone along with learning her rather extravagant choreography. They'd practiced in her room, knocking books off the shelves and making a general racket, until Lou had insisted they "rehearse" (as Vi called it) in the back yard.

At Homecoming that year, the D.J. had thrown in some swing music—Kade assumed because of the theme—and Vi had dragged him out onto the dance floor. He would never have admitted it, but it was one of the highlights of his high school career.

And one of the worst nights of his life. Because it was during that dance that he realized he'd fallen for his best friend . . . his best friend who was undeniably in love with Liam Durant.

"Come on," Vi said pleadingly, reaching for him again. "Just a little bit. For old time's sake?"

Kade rolled his head back, eyes on the ceiling. What was he thinking? He shouldn't even be considering this. It was silly. It was unprofessional. It was—

"Please?" Vi begged, hands clasped before her.

Kade sighed and took her left hand in his, slipped his left around her waist. "I can't believe I'm doing this," he mumbled. "If anyone sees—"

"No one's gonna see!" Vi looked around quickly, just to make sure. "Now a one, and a two, and a—"

They started in on the familiar steps. It had been more than ten years, but they'd done it so many times it came back to him instinctively. He twirled her away, then back again and Vi's smile was infectious.

"Come on now," she said, matching his steps. "Do the flip!"

Without even thinking, he grabbed her around the waist with one hand, and under the knees with the other, flipping her over. She landed on her feet and bounced up onto her toes. With a laugh, she threw her arms around his neck.

"We've still got it," she said, looking up at him, her blue eyes shining.

Kade's own hands were around her waist, under her coat, the fabric of her sweater soft beneath his fingers. He inhaled sharply and smelled that vanilla flowers scent again, clean and fresh and warm.

His stomach flipped, and Kade froze. What was he doing?

He stepped back, sliding his hands into his pockets. Why were they trembling? Probably because this was a horrible idea. Anyone coming in could have seen them and easily drawn the wrong conclusions. It was so unprofessional. So inappropriate.

They weren't kids anymore.

"Hey, are you okay?" Violet asked softly. She went to touch his arm, but he jerked back and she looked stricken. "Kade, what's wrong?"

"Sorry." He rubbed a hand over his face. "Sorry, nothing. It's just . . . we probably shouldn't be doing this at school, you know? It's not exactly professional."

Light dawned on Vi's face. "I didn't even—" She took a step back herself. "Sorry. I shouldn't have—"

"It's okay—"

"No, it's not. I didn't think—"

"Vi, it's *fine*." Kade grabbed her shoulders, squeezed them once, then let go. "Seriously, it's no big deal. We should probably get to class, though. School starts in half an hour."

Vi nodded. "You're right. And now, I'm freaking out about facing a room full of sixteen-year olds."

"Some are seventeen," he offered.

"Not helping." She smiled at him, though. "Drama and music still down that way?" she asked, indicating the hall behind her with a thumb.

"Yep. I'm the other direction," he said, backing away. "See you at lunch?"

"In the faculty break room," she said, forcing a note of awe into her voice as she walked backward, too. "I finally get to see it."

"It is pretty amazing."

"It's a thing of *legend*," she said. "Is it true you have cupcakes *every day*?"

"I guess you'll just have to wait and see!"

"I can't wait." Vi grinned, adjusting her own bag

over her shoulder. "How do I look?" she asked, holding her hands out to her sides.

"Ready to mold young minds."

"Now that's a frightening thought," she said, widening her eyes and forcing her mouth into a comical frown. "See ya!" And with that, she turned on her heel and headed down the hall.

Kade did not watch her go. Well, not any longer than would be completely normal and appropriate, that is.

A freckled girl with curly red hair raised her hand.

"Yes?" Vi consulted her class seating chart. "Madison?"

"It's Madi," she corrected. "Will this be on the test?"

Violet tried not to roll her eyes at the girl. "We're simply reading through the first act to get a feel for the language," she said. "Shakespeare's writing has a certain rhythm."

Madi narrowed her eyes. "So it *won't* be on the test?" She relaxed a bit into her seat.

Oh no you don't.

Vi arched a brow. "Anything we discuss in class

could be on the test. You never know." She ignored the chorus of groans.

Another hand shot up, and she glanced down at the list again. "Andrew?"

"Is it true you were a movie star?" Whispers broke out around him and the boy grinned, the cowlick on the back of his head bouncing.

"No, I was not a movie star."

"She wouldn't be *here* if she was a movie star," a blonde girl—Taylor—scoffed. "Idiot!"

"You're an idiot!"

"Shut up!"

"All right, that's enough!" Vi raised her voice to be heard over the escalating din. "Quiet down unless you want detention!"

That threat seemed to work as well as it ever did. The noise quieted a bit, but for a disgruntled rumble, which she ignored.

"I was a working actress, in New York, for the past few years," she said. "I was in some plays, a few commercials . . ."

"You were on TV?" Taylor perked up, already pulling out her phone. "What commercial? I want to find it on YouTube—"

"Phones away," Vi ordered. Taylor wrinkled her nose but obeyed.

"I'll be happy to discuss my career at another time," she said. "For now, back to *Taming of the Shrew*, please."

More grumbles, and just when Petruchio announced his intention to woo Katarina, the bell rang.

"Don't forget the assigned reading tonight!" she shouted out over the kids filing out. They weren't listening, of course.

Vi collapsed into her seat, exhausted.

And that was only first period.

The next class filed in and she got to her feet. Tomorrow, she was definitely wearing flats.

"Hello, class, I'm Miss Chalmers, your new teacher," she said. "How about some Shakespeare?"

The class groaned.

It was going to be a long day.

She made it through the rest of her classes, had lunch in the faculty lounge—no cupcakes. Kade was a big, fat liar—and emerged into the parking lot after school relatively unscathed.

Well, her feet hurt and her voice was a little

raspy, but other than that, it went pretty well, she thought.

"You survived!" Kade called out as she approached. He was leaning insouciantly against the hood of his car, looking way less tired than Vi felt.

"Three drama classes and two choirs, thank you very much," she said with a little bow. "How are you so relaxed? Math must be much way easier to teach."

He snorted. "That must be it."

"I'm serious," she said as they got in the car. "I mean, you give 'em a textbook, assign 'em thirty problems. Done. You can sit back and play solitaire the rest of the hour."

Kade gave her a wry look. "Solitaire? I'm not eighty."

"Whatever," she said, too tired to argue. "I just want to take a nice, hot bath and—"

"Grade papers?" he suggested.

She made a face. "You're no fun."

"I take offense at that," he retorted. He turned out of the parking lot and headed down the street. "I am an *immense* amount of fun. And I know exactly what you need right now." He held up a finger when she opened her mouth. "It's not a bath," he said.

She frowned. "I can't imagine what would be better than a bath."

He turned onto Main Street and passed the town square. "You sure?" The corner of his mouth quirked up.

Vi turned in her seat to study him. "What are you up to?" she asked slowly. Then she looked out the windshield, scanning their surroundings.

"Oh!" she said suddenly. "You mean—"

He nodded.

"It's still here?"

Kade grinned. "Of course."

They pulled to a stop along the curb, and Vi looked up at the store front before her. A green and white striped awning shaded the wide front window, but she could still read the gold-painted letters: *McKenna's Creamery*. She gave a little gasp. McKenna's had the best ice cream in the state . . . in the *world*. Probably in the universe.

"Are you coming in?" Kade asked. He was standing beside the car, poking his head back in. "Or are you going to stare longingly at it all day?"

Vi scrambled for the door handle. "I'm coming!"

A rush of nostalgia hit her when she opened the front door. Warm, sugar cone scented air washed over her face as a bell rang overhead.

"Be right with you!" a voice called from behind a curtained doorway. The shop was empty—no big surprise on a freezing Monday afternoon in February.

Vi took in the black and white tile floor, the pale turquoise walls . . . the gleaming wooden counter and spinning barstools. "It looks exactly the same," she murmured.

"Nothing changes in HJ, you know that," Kade said, approaching the glass-fronted cases. "I think it's in the town charter."

Vi climbed onto one of the stools and gave it a spin. "Remember that time we challenged each other to see who could eat a Colossal and spin the longest without getting sick?"

Kade made a face. "I do," he said. "I lost."

Vi laughed and spun around again. "That you did."

The curtain parted and a young woman walked out. "Sorry to keep you waiting," she said, wiping her hands on a towel. She was tall and lithe with long brown hair and dimples creasing her cheeks as she smiled at them. A smile that was very familiar.

"Oh my—" Vi stood up and nearly stumbled over the stool. "Lena?"

"Vi?" The dimples deepened. "I didn't know you were in town! How are you?" She rounded the counter and took Vi in a tight hug. "It's so good to see you!"

"Same here." Vi pulled back. "You look just the same. What are you doing here? Last I heard you'd left town and were in Australia or something."

"I was." She walked back behind the counter. "I spent a few years backpacking through Europe, doing odd jobs. Went to Australia, New Zealand, Bali—"

"Sounds amazing."

"It was," she said. "But after a while I got homesick, you know?"

Vi didn't, but she didn't say that. "And you're working here? In high school you hated it."

Lena shrugged. "Things change. My dad got older and he was thinking about selling the shop, but —" She held out her hands. "So here I am, the fourth McKenna to run McKenna's Creamery." She glanced toward Kade. "I see some things don't change. You two were always joined at the hip."

"We were not—" Kade began.

"I don't think—" Vi said at the same time.

Lena laughed. "Two peas in a pod," she said. "Well, what can I get you? Two Colossals?" She waggled her eyebrows at Kade. "Think you can handle it, big guy?"

Kade grimaced. "I think I'll just take a scoop of peanut butter chocolate in a sugar cone."

"And I'll do . . ." Vi perused the buckets behind the glass. "A scoop of pistachio and a scoop of rocky road."

"A double?" Kade's eyebrows shot up.

"Hey, I deserve it after today." She caught Lena's eye. "My first day teaching at the high school," she explained.

"My condolences." She handed Kade his cone and started on Vi's. "Does that mean you'll be here for a while?"

"Yeah, at least a year or so," Vi replied. "Then back to New York, or maybe L.A."

Lena piled on the second scoop. "The glamorous life."

The bell rang over the door and Vi glanced over her shoulder to see a group of teenagers coming in.

"Here you go," Lena said, handing Vi her cone. "On the house, to welcome you home."

"Oh, you don't have to—"

"I know I don't *have* to." Lena's dimples flashed. "But I *want* to. And you and I need to get together and catch up. Soon."

"Sounds good," Vi said, licking her cone as the kids flooded over, perusing the ice cream choices.

They sat at a table instead of the bar—they were grownups now, after all. And the kids took all the barstools. Vi savored her ice cream, unable to keep from making little noises of appreciation.

"Why is it so good?" she asked, wiping her mouth.

"Fresh, local ingredients mixed with love," Kade replied, reciting the shop's tagline.

"Yeah, well, I don't buy it," she said, taking a large bite and talking through a mouthful of deliciousness. "There has to be something illegal in here."

Kade pointed toward Lena, with her All-American, fresh-faced, nice-girl-next-doorness. "You really think Lena McKenna is drugging the good people of Holiday Junction?"

Vi narrowed her eyes as if considering it. "It's always the ones you least suspect."

Kade bit into his sugar cone. "She does seem awfully happy." He said it as if it were a crime.

"Almost . . . *too* happy, I'd say." Vi nodded sagely.

Kade snorted.

"I can't believe she traveled all over the world and ended up right back here," Vi said. "How about you? Did you ever have the urge to shake the dust of HJ off your feet and see the world?"

Kade shrugged. "I went to college."

"In *Seattle,*" she said. "That's three hours away!"

"I like it here," he said, popping the last of his cone in his mouth and crunching loudly.

Vi studied him. "You never had the urge to try to be a musician? You were so good."

"I'm *still* good," Kade said with a sniff. "And I play music. I teach. I write."

"But you don't want to record an album? Go on tour?" she prodded.

"Not everyone wants to be famous," he said, a little shortly. "I've sold a few of my songs, actually."

"You did?" Vi was surprised she didn't know this. "Anything I would have heard?"

He shrugged. "Maybe. You ever hear *Dancing on Water?*"

Vi gasped. "By Kellie Kincaid?"

"Well, Kellie Kincaid sang it, but it's *by* Kade Rivera."

"No way!" Vi's ice cream dripped onto the table, forgotten. "You wrote that? It was a huge hit!"

He looked down, his cheeks reddening. "Yeah, it did all right."

"All right? That song was so good—so catchy."

"Thanks."

"Did you write any others?" she asked, finally remembering to lick her ice cream.

He looked decidedly uncomfortable. It was so like Kade not to want to toot his own horn. "I've sold a few to Kellie, a few to that group out of the U.K, London Eye. One to Eddie Macaren."

Vi sat back, stunned. "I can't believe this. You're like a famous songwriter and I had absolutely no idea."

"I'm not famous," he protested.

"And you're still teaching high school?" she asked. "Why?"

"I like it," he replied with a shrug. "I like teaching math, and I like teaching guitar, and I like living in Holiday Junction and writing songs."

"Huh." That was all she could say. It was like Kade was suddenly this entirely different person and she didn't know him at all.

"Your ice cream," Kade said, startling her. When she looked at him blankly, he added, "You're making a mess. Sheesh, Chalmers, you leave town for a few years and when you come back, you don't even know how to eat ice cream? What did they do to you in New York?"

And he was back. The Kade she knew. She

swiped at the melted ice cream with a napkin and got up to throw the rest away.

"So, really. How did it go today?" Kade asked, following her to the trash can to throw away his own mess. "You think you'll stick with it?"

"I don't really have a choice," Vi admitted. "But yeah, I will. Some of the kids are a bit challenging, but most of them are pretty great."

"Yeah, they are."

"And my Advanced Choir is amazing," she said. "Some real talent in there."

"They did a great job at the fall concert," he told her. "When do you start rehearsals for the spring musical?"

"We'll do the first read-through tomorrow. I met some of the cast in my classes today and they seem pretty excited." She grinned at him. "It's always been my dream to direct."

"Watch out Steven Spielberg." He held the door open for her.

She waved goodbye to Lena before walking out. "Like *Spielberg* could handle a high school production of *The Music Man*."

Kade laughed as they crossed the sidewalk, heading to the car.

He had a nice laugh.

Well, that was a weird thought. She'd never noticed Kade's laugh before . . . well, at least not in a way to say if it was nice or not nice, or whatever. But for some reason, it hit her differently in that moment, the glint of his teeth, the sparkle in his eyes . . . the way he shook his head like he found her utterly charming.

Okay. Definitely weird.

"Violet? Violet Chalmers?" A masculine voice had Vi stopping in her tracks. She turned around and couldn't hold back a little gasp.

Liam Durant.

Four

Liam Durant.

Kade had never had any hard feelings toward Liam. He was a pretty nice guy, all things considered. But suddenly, he had the urge to punch Liam right in the face, and he had no idea why. Kade took a deep breath, hanging back a little as Violet hugged him.

"I—I can't believe you're here," she said, stepping back. "How are you?"

Liam smiled and swept a hand over his neatly brushed, sandy hair. He wore a tailored dark suit and overcoat with a dark red tie. Kade couldn't help comparing it to his own jeans, boots, and gray wool sweater.

"I'm fine. Good," Liam said, and it was obvious he bore no ill will toward Vi for dumping him. He subtly took her in, his eyes raking over her when her gaze dropped to the ground at her feet.

"How have you been?" he asked. "When did you get back?"

She looked back up at him, her cheeks pink. "Just this weekend," she said. "I'm doing well. Moved home for a while and I'm teaching at the high school." She tucked a lock of golden hair behind her ear, smiling up at him.

Why was he so tall?

Why did that irritate Kade so much?

"That's great!" Liam said, his smile widening. He leaned toward her, his head tilted down, and it was like the two of them were in their own little world. "It's really good to see you."

"You, too." She chewed on her bottom lip.

And that was about enough of that. Kade stepped closer, until he was right next to Vi. "How's it going, Liam?" he asked, holding out a hand.

Liam looked surprised but shook his hand. "Hey, Kade. Fine. You?"

"Fine." Kade might have put a little extra muscle in the handshake, but Liam didn't seem to notice. Or if he did, he didn't say anything about it.

"Wow, it's like old times." Liam pulled back his hand when Kade released it and stuck it in his pants pocket. Then he startled and checked his watch.

"Oh man, I have to go," he said. "I have an appointment."

"Oh, sure." Vi tried to hide it, but Kade could tell she was disappointed. "It was nice to see you."

Liam hesitated, then seemed to square his shoulders, bracing himself for something. "We should get together and catch up," he said to Vi. "Dinner sometime, maybe?"

Vi practically beamed. "That would be great. Perfect!"

Liam pulled out his phone, and Vi gave him her number. He seemed like he was going to say something else, but he shook his head.

"I'm sorry. I've really got to go," he said, starting off down the sidewalk before he spun around, walking backward. "I'll call you."

"You better!" Vi called back, and he whirled around and walked quickly away. Vi watched him go with a faraway look on her face.

It was like high school all over again. "Seriously?" Kade muttered under his breath, and Vi elbowed him.

"*You better*!" he mimicked, and she glared at him.

"Shut up."

"Oh, *Liam*!" He fluttered his eyelashes. "You're so *dreamy!*"

"Oh for—" She shoved him toward the car. "Can we go, please?"

"His *eyes!* And that *smile!*"

"That's it, I'm walking home," Vi said, pushing him again. "On second thought, I'm taking your keys and *you're* walking home!"

Kade laughed and rounded the car, unlocking the doors. "You couldn't handle this car."

Vi eyed it, and Kade knew what she saw: A ten-year-old hatchback with a dent in the back quarter panel.

"You're right." She nodded somberly. "This is way too much machine for me."

Kade laughed and got in the car.

They took off on the short ride toward home; Vi leaning her head on the passenger window and staring out silently.

"So—" Kade cleared his throat, suddenly nervous. "You and Liam?"

She glanced over at him. "What about us?"

Us. Were they an *us* already?

"You really think you want to—I don't know—start things up again?"

"No." Vi laughed, shaking her head. "Yes. I don't know. Maybe?"

"That's a lot of options."

She rolled her eyes. "It was nice to see him again.

There seems to be *something* there . . . maybe. So, I don't know. I guess . . . maybe?"

He arched a brow. "So definitely *maybe*."

She scrunched up her nose, looking at him sideways. "Is it weird?"

Kade wasn't sure what to say to that. In fact, he did think it was a little weird. But Vi was his friend, so . . .

"Not weird," he replied slowly, turning the corner onto their street. "But it has been a long time. You've changed. He's changed."

"I know that."

"You can't go back to high school," he said.

She huffed out a laugh. "I definitely know *that*." Vi shook her head. "It's just dinner. He might not even call."

Kade snorted. "Oh, he'll definitely call."

She bit her lip. "You think?"

"I take back what I said about going back to high school." Kade sighed heavily. "Yes. He'll call. He likes you. He *likes* you, likes you."

Vi smacked him on the arm. Did she hit him this much in high school? He didn't remember.

"Well, I could do worse," Vi said after a moment. "He's a good guy. Stable. Reliable."

"Boring." Why did he say that?

"I doubt that," Vi said, turning in the seat to face him, one leg tucked under the other. "But I've been with *fun* guys. *Spontaneous* guys. Ben was fun and he—" She leaned her head back against the seat, closing her eyes. "There's something to be said for boring and reliable. Someone you can trust."

Kade turned into his driveway and pulled to a stop. "It's not one or the other, you know," he said quietly. "You could have it all."

Vi said nothing but tipped her head a little in acknowledgment before she got out of the car. "Thanks for the ride."

"No problem. See you in the morning?"

She nodded and headed up the front steps of her house.

Kade watched her go, uncertain why his stomach felt heavy as a rock.

"I'm home," Vi called out as she kicked off her boots and hung her coat by the front door. "Mom?"

"Back here!"

She followed the voice to the kitchen and took a seat at the counter, sneaking a cookie from the cookie jar while her mom wasn't looking. Lou stood at the stove, staring warily at a pot bubbling away. Vi sniffed, unable to recognize the scent.

"What are you making?" she asked. There was a cooled pie crust sitting next to the stove, along with a can of tuna, mayonnaise, and an empty box of . . . was that lemon Jell-O?

"I'm not sure," Lou replied. "It's called Summer Salad Pie. The book club wanted a sixties vintage theme this month, so I'm trying out some recipes." She poured boiling water into a bowl. "This one seems questionable, but it won some baking contest back in the day." She slowly stirred what was in the bowl, and Vi could smell lemons. So that explained the Jell-O.

"Why aren't you at the store?" Vi asked.

Lou poured tomato sauce and vinegar into the bowl. "Charlie's closing tonight."

"Charlie?"

Her mom gave her a puzzled look. "I told you about Charlie, didn't I? High school kid who works in the afternoons?" When Vi shrugged, Lou kept stirring, pouring some Worcestershire sauce into the bowl. "Anyway, he's a nice kid. Hard worker. And it gives me time to do other things." She added a splash of Tabasco, and Vi grimaced.

"Okay, what *is* that? It looks disgusting."

Lou gave the bowl a sniff. "Lemon tomato gelatin filling," she said, mixing in a pile of chopped celery, onions, and olives. She crossed the room and put it all in the refrigerator. "It has to chill for a bit, want to help me with the tuna salad for the top?"

Vi kind of thought the idea of tuna salad was the revolting cherry on top of the rather horrifying cake —or pie—but she shrugged and opened the can of tuna while her mom started in on the dishes.

"So how was your first day?" her mom asked.

Vi checked the recipe and added some celery and onions. "Pretty good, I think," she replied. "A few hiccups, but overall it went well. Oh, Kade took me to McKenna's afterward—"

"Oh yeah?" She shot her a glance that Vi couldn't really read.

"What?"

Lou turned back to the dishes. "Nothing."

Vi let it go. "Anyway, I saw Lena. We're going to get together soon and catch up."

Lou dried her hands. "Oh, that's nice. She's such a sweet girl."

Vi glopped in some mayonnaise. "And then as we were leaving, I ran into Liam Durant." As she said his name, a rush of butterflies took flight in her stomach.

"Oh really?" And what was that tone?

"What is that tone?" she asked as Lou went to the fridge and pulled out the tomato bowl.

"No tone," Lou replied, holding the bowl out to Vi as she moved the spoon through it. "Does that look partially thickened to you?"

It looked terrible to her, but she shrugged. "I guess."

Lou nodded, poured the concoction into the pie crust, and put it back in the fridge. "So how was Liam?"

"Fine." Her stomach flipped again.

"Fine?"

Vi gave the tuna a final stir and pushed the bowl away. "Yes. Fine. Why?"

Lou's eyes narrowed and she leaned across the counter, studying her daughter. "What's up with you?"

"Nothing."

"Mm hmm . . ." She stood up straight, but didn't let up with her penetrating gaze. "What happened with Liam?"

"Nothing *happened* with Liam," she said, eyes dropping to the countertop. Why did she feel like she was fifteen again? "He just said we should have dinner sometime."

"And you want to have dinner with him?"

"Sure. Yes. Why not? Why is everyone being so weird about this?"

"Who is being weird about it?"

"You. Kade." Vi threw up her hands. "We're old friends and we *might* have dinner. What's the big deal?"

Lou crossed her arms over her chest. "Kade was weird about it?"

"Yeah, he was all *you could have it all*, whatever that means," she replied, irritated. "Like I'm planning to *marry* the guy or something."

"Huh." Lou tapped a finger on her chin.

"Huh, what?"

Lou shook her head. "Nothing. Just thinking."

"See?" She pointed at her mother. "Case in point. *Weird*."

Her mom smiled slightly. "Honey, we just want to make sure you know what you're doing. That you don't rush into anything. After everything you went through with Ben—"

"This has *nothing* to do with Ben!"

"Doesn't it?"

Violet pressed her lips together and looked away. She didn't want to think about Ben. About . . . all of it. Lou reached across the counter to touch her arm.

"I'm not telling you what to do," she said quietly. "I only want you to be careful. I don't want you to get hurt."

The fight went out of Vi at her mother's earnest expression. "I know."

"All I want—All I've *ever* wanted was for you to be happy."

She slumped a little more. "I know, Mom."

Lou patted her arm and pulled back, taking the tuna bowl with her and putting it in the refrigerator.

"It's probably nothing, anyway," Vi said, hooking her feet around the legs of the barstool and swiveling it a little. "Just old friends having dinner. He might not even call—" At that, Vi's cell phone rang.

Her mother closed the fridge door, her brows shooting up. "You were saying?"

Vi checked the unknown number on the phone screen. "It's probably not even him. Probably a telemarketer," she said, answering the call. "Hello?"

"Vi? It's Liam."

"Oh . . . hi!" She glanced at her mother, who mouthed *telemarketer* at her with a smug expression on her face. Vi got up and went into the living room. "Hi, Liam. How's it going?"

How's it going? Who said that? She might as well have said '*Sup*?

"Um, good. It's going good," he replied. "Look, I was wondering if you were free for dinner Friday night."

Vi's stomach started its butterfly thing again. "Friday? Sure. I can do Friday." She toyed with her hair, then realized she was doing it and jerked her hand down.

"I'll pick you up around six?"

"Sure. That sounds great!" Man, she was over-doing the perky. She took a deep breath and willed her racing heart to slow. "Six is fine."

"Okay, perfect," he said, and she could hear the smile in his voice. "I'm looking forward to it."

"Me, too."

"See you soon, Vi. Bye."

"Bye." She hung up and took a deep breath, letting it out slowly.

"How's Liam?" Lou called from the kitchen.

Vi rolled her eyes. "Fine, Mom." She looked out the front window and spotted Kade getting his mail.

She smirked, a rather evil thought coming to mind. "Hey, Mom, when's that pie going to be ready?"

"About an hour, why?"

"No reason." She slipped on her boots and opened the front door, calling out to Kade as he climbed his own front steps. He paused, one foot on the porch as she approached.

"Hey," she said, a little out of breath. "You want to come to dinner in about an hour?"

Kade slapped the pile of mail on his thigh. "Sure. Can I bring anything?"

Vi thought of the gross tomato tuna pie in the fridge. "Nah, just your appetite!"

An hour later, Kade stared down at the jiggling red mass on his plate. "So . . . new recipe?"

Vi valiantly fought off the urge to laugh. "Mom's testing it out for the book club."

He shot a glance toward the kitchen door, where Lou had disappeared a moment earlier to get more napkins. "Is she plotting their demise?"

Vi choked on a giggle as her mother came back in and plopped a pile of paper napkins in the middle of the table. "How is it?" she asked them.

Vi forked up a piece of the pie. It shook a little on her fork, the red tomato layer glistening and pocked with pieces of pimento-stuffed olives. "Just about to try it," she said. "Kade's really excited."

Kade shot her a glare, then smoothed his expression into a smile when Lou looked over at him. He cut off a piece of the pie. "Looks delicious," he said.

He hesitated, and Vi's lips twitched. "Well, eat it," she said.

"Oh, you first." He grinned at her.

Vi was up for the challenge. "We'll try it at the same time," she said.

Kade arched a brow. Challenge accepted. "Okay, then. One . . ."

"Two . . ." Vi joined in.

"Three!" They both shoved the forkfuls of pie into their mouths and chewed.

Oh, the humanity.

The tuna part wasn't bad, really. And combined with the cheesy crust, it would have been like a flaky tuna sandwich, if not for the tomato layer.

The lemon jello, vinegar, Worcestershire, onion, olive, Tabasco, tomato layer that launched the Summer Salad Pie from the land of *Kind of Weird* into the stratosphere of *Why Would Someone DO This?*

"Well, don't keep me in suspense," Lou said. "What do you think?"

Vi noticed that her mom hadn't taken a bite yet and forced herself to swallow and smile. "It's delicious."

Kade started to say something, but she kicked

him under the table. He caught on quickly, though. That was one thing about Kade.

"It really is," he said, nodding. "I thought it would be weird, but it's really not." He cut off another piece and shoved it in his mouth. "Yummy!" he said through a mouthful of gelatinous ooze.

Kade was nothing if not committed to seeing things through.

"Really?" Lou looked equal parts surprised and pleased. She cut off a large forkful of pie and lifted it to her lips. Vi held her breath as her mom put it in her mouth, chewed once, then froze, her eyes widening.

Vi snickered as she watched her grabbed a handful of napkins and spit the mess out.

"That is *horrible!*" Lou gulped down some water and set her glass down with a thunk as Vi and Kade laughed hysterically. "And you're both horrible, too!"

The Summer Salad Pie went into the trash, Kade ordered pizza, and they spent a pleasant evening laughing and watching the British Baking Show on TV.

And it was only late that night, right before she fell asleep, that Vi remembered she had a date with Liam on Friday night.

She drifted off before she could think about how weird it was that she'd forgotten.

While Violet lay sleeping, Lou stared up at the ceiling in her own room, deep in thought. After a while, she texted her friend Anne.

You awake?

A response came almost immediately. *Of course. Why should my brain let me sleep in the middle of the night?*

Lou smirked and pushed the call button.

"What's up?" Anne asked on a yawn.

Lou considered what she was about to do. "I may need your help."

"Oh yeah, with what?" Lou could hear Anne sitting up in bed. "You need to dispose of a body?"

Lou snorted. "You know you'd be my first call, but no," she said. "It's Vi."

"Vi? What's wrong with Vi?"

She sighed. "Well, you know that . . . *Ben* . . . really did a number on her."

"I know, sweetie," she said sympathetically.

"I think she might need some help digging herself out of that slump."

"Oh yeah?" Anne's voice perked up. "Is this a job for the Mamas?"

"I think it could very well be," Lou replied. "Can you meet at the *Grind* for coffee tomorrow morning?"

Anne hummed for a moment, considering. "I can probably get away once the shop opens for a bit. Sam will take care of things."

"Okay, that would be great. I'll text Mandy and see you there." Lou paused for a moment. "Thanks."

"Oh, you know I live for this," Anne said, and Lou could hear the smile in her voice. "Good night."

"Night!"

Lou hung up and tossed her phone onto the nightstand. Then, confident she had the situation well in hand, she rolled over and finally went to sleep.

Five

The next morning, Lou and Anne sat at a small table in the *Daily Grind*, sipping cappuccinos while Lou watched the bookstore through the arched doorway between the two shops. She was alone in the store in the mornings, but Tuesdays were pretty slow anyway. Mandy, on the other hand, had been making coffee since they arrived; a line of customers steadily drifting in. Her early morning barista had called in sick, and she was on her own until relief arrived.

Finally, around ten, the replacement barista arrived, and Mandy collapsed into a seat with a sigh. "I'm getting too old for this," she moaned, running her hands over the multitude of salt-and-pepper braids gathered at her nape with an elastic band. Her warm, brown skin glistened from the steam of the espresso machine.

"Oh, don't be silly," Lou said. "You're younger than either of us."

"Is forty-nine too early to retire?" she asked.

"Yes," the other two said simultaneously.

"Okay, enough about that," Anne said, adjusting her brown ponytail. She was dressed in a *Holiday Junction Bakery* t-shirt and jeans. A fine dusting of flour coated her clothing and she peered at Lou through her glasses. "What's up with Vi?"

"Yeah, what is up with Vi?" Mandy asked, her dark eyes thoughtful. "Everybody's been wondering why she's back in town."

"She's back to teach school and save up some money," Lou replied. "But that's not why I asked you both to come here."

They leaned forward, arms crossed on the table. "Well, what is it?"

Lou pursed her lips. "Vi is a bit lost," she replied. "Things didn't work out in New York how she hoped, career-wise. And then this mess with Ben—"

Both ladies offered very unladylike curses at the mention of his name.

"Yes, well . . ." Lou's lips quirked at their defense of her daughter. "It's been a while since he left, and I think Vi's ready to get back into the game, so to speak. But it has to be the right guy."

Anne and Mandy exchanged a glance. "Mamas," they said with a nod.

Lou smiled.

In addition to running local businesses, being on the Chamber of Commerce, and organizing town events, Anne, Mandy, and Lou had another hobby. They'd all found their soul mates early in life. Like Lou, Mandy was a widow, her husband, Kurt, killed in a car accident about five years ago, leaving her a single mom to their then-nineteen-year-old twins. Anne and Sam were still happily married, after thirty-some years, with four grown children of their own.

One of the things that made the women such close friends was their belief in love. All-encompassing, real, true, love.

And they loved to help others find it.

They seemed to have a knack for it, too. Although none of their kids were married—yet—they had brought together John and Sue Jackson . . . and the Bailey boy and that lovely girl, Annette, were engaged to be married the following June. In fact, they had brought together so many couples, the group had been dubbed the Matchmaking Mamas.

No one said it to their faces, of course, but they knew. And the three women actually liked it.

"So . . . do you have someone in mind for Vi?" Anne asked, scratching her nose and leaving a little flour behind.

Lou folded her hands, resting her chin on them. “It appears she's thinking about starting things up with Liam Durant again.”

“Oh, well, he's a good choice.” Anne leaned back in her chair. “Nice boy. Good job. And they were so cute when they were together back in school.”

Lou said nothing, and Mandy studied her closely.

“You're not happy about Liam?” she asked.

“No, it's not that,” Lou replied. “Liam's a very nice boy. It's just—”

“Just—” they said in unison.

Lou toyed with her ~~with~~ coffee cup, spinning it around on the table. “I think she may be settling for what's safe. What's familiar, you know? She has such good memories with Liam, and I'm sure over the years she's wondered what might have been.”

“Who doesn't?” Mandy asked.

Lou tipped her head in agreement. “I only want to make sure she doesn't rush into something because it's comfortable. Because it's expected. And I want her to know that she has other options.”

“Anyone specific in mind?” Anne asked, and Lou could tell by the way she asked the question, that she already knew the answer.

Lou smiled slowly. “Maybe,” she replied.

"Vi won't be happy if she knows we've been meddling," Mandy pointed out.

"Then she better not find out," Lou said. "And we're not *meddling*. We're simply going to help her see that Liam Durant isn't the only game in town."

"We won't try to steer her one way or the other," Anne said slowly. "Just make sure she has all she needs to make an informed choice."

Mandy snorted. "You make it sound like choosing a life insurance policy."

"It is, in a way," Lou said.

"Oh! Oh!" Anne bounced up and down a little. "It's *love* insurance!" She grinned at them in triumph, only to be met by groans.

"What?" she said, hurt. "I thought it was clever."

"It was, sweetie," Lou said, patting her arm. "Now, I have a few ideas, and I'm going to need your help—both of you."

They leaned in across the table and plotted and planned—and across town at Holiday Junction High School, Vi was none the wiser.

Violet thought Tuesday went better than Monday. Her students seemed to listen to her, she gave a pop quiz and only got minimal push-back, and after school, she had her first read-through of the spring musical. Her lead actors were very good, in Vi's opinion, but she was waiting until they started rehearsing the songs to get her hopes up. The Music Man could be a tough show, with lots of tongue-twisting lyrics and quick scene changes, and she hoped the kids were up for the challenge. They assured her they were.

She'd ridden to school with Kade again, but since she had to stay after, she ended up walking over to *Chalmers' Chapters* to catch a ride home with her mom. She paused a moment before going into the shop, looking at the familiar sign hanging overhead, the dark blue, carved wooden door, and the display of books in the window. Her mom had already set up for Valentine's Day, with vases of roses, heart-shaped confetti, and a vast array of romantic novels. A hanging banner read *Fall in Love with Reading* in sparkling red letters.

Vi walked in, shoving the door a little hard out of habit—it had always stuck a bit—and inhaled the familiar scent of old leather and worn pages. She'd always loved the bookstore. Her earliest memories were of hiding out under the front counter, playing with toys, or running down the narrow aisles, the bookshelves towering above her all the way to the ceiling. It had seemed so big to her back then—a supply of books so endless that no one could possibly read them all.

Mom had moved things around a bit. A grouping of four worn leather chairs around a small table created a reading nook off to the left, and the children's section was now upstairs in the loft, a large, bright yellow arrow pointing the way up. Everything else was the same, though—the shelves crammed with used paperbacks, the table piled with donated books waiting to be put into the system . . . the arched doorway on the right leading to the coffee shop next door.

"Well, hey you!" Her mother walked in from the back, a stack of hardbacks in her arms. She set them carefully on the counter. "I was wondering when you'd find your way over here."

"I just finished with rehearsal," she replied, grabbing a piece of candy out of the dish next to the cash register. "Was hoping I could ride home with you?"

"Of course." Lou flipped open one of the books and made a note on a yellow legal pad. "I'll be closing early today anyway for the town meeting."

"There's a town meeting?" Vi chewed on the candy, the peppermint crunching loudly.

Her mom slammed the book shut and picked up another. "Joshua called an emergency meeting. I swear, that man calls more emergency meetings . . ." She made another note and opened the next book. "Probably going to be a waste of time."

"So don't go," Vi suggested with a shrug.

The look her mom gave her made Vi feel like she'd threatened to burn the place down.

"I *have* to go," Lou said slowly. "I'm on the Chamber of Commerce. I'm head of the planning committee. If I don't go, who knows what he'll do." She finished with her pile of books and set them aside. "Someone has to keep him in line."

"Sorry." Vi held up her hands defensively.

"You know what happened last time I missed a meeting?" her mom asked, really getting worked up now. "We had white poinsettias on the gazebo steps instead of red. White poinsettias!"

Vi wasn't sure why that was a problem. "White poinsettias are pretty."

Her mom glared at her. "The *gazebo* is white. The poinsettias were completely washed out!" She started unpacking a box of bookmarks and putting them into a display rack. "There's a reason we always have red. Contrast. Contrast is key!" She waved a handful of bookmarks at Vi to emphasize the point.

"Of course." Vi eyed her mom carefully. "We wouldn't want a repeat of the Great White Poinsettia Scandal."

Her mom harrumphed in agreement. "You're coming, right?"

"Me? Why do I have to go?" Vi did not sound like a petulant teenager in that moment. She *didn't*.

"To back me up, of course."

"You need *me* for backup? How about Mandy or Anne?" Her mom's two closest friends also owned businesses in HJ and were just as involved in the town's holiday planning.

"Oh, they try, but they're weak," Lou said, waving a hand. "When Joshua goes after them, they fold like a cheap suit."

"Which is an odd phrase, because wouldn't any suit fold? Cheap or not?" Vi took another piece of candy. "I mean, all you have to do is, you know, fold it." She unwrapped the peppermint and popped it in her mouth, hoping her comment would distract her mother.

It didn't. "You need to come with me."

"I mean, it would be *hard* to fold, obviously," Vi said, pretending not to hear.

"Vi—"

"Because it's a suit. Kind of bulky. But not *impossible*, is what I'm saying."

"Violet!" Her mother propped her fists on her hips and gave her that mom look. The I-birthed-you-and-you-owe-me look. The if-you-don't-I'll-guilt-you-for-the-rest-of-your-life look.

Vi folded. Like a cheap suit. "Fine. I'll go."

The Holiday Junction town meetings were held in the gym-slash-cafeteria of Holiday Junction Elementary School—a large beigey-gray room with basketball hoops folded up against the ceiling, and a stage at one end where they performed concerts and the annual talent show.

It smelled vaguely of cheese.

Vi sat in a metal folding chair next to Lou, near the middle of the room. Lou had wanted to sit in the front row, but Vi had talked her out of it. Or rather, she'd just kept talking until Lou finally gave up. Lou's closest friends, Mandy and Anne, sat across the aisle. Mandy Klein ran the *Daily Grind*, the coffee shop adjacent to *Chapters*, and Anne Patterson owned the *Holiday Junction Bakery* on the other end of town. Together, the three were a force to be reckoned with. An organizational machine that kept the town's holiday celebrations on track. A whirling dervish of glitter, twinkle lights, and comfortable shoes.

The seats filled quickly—Vi waved to Lena, who was sitting near the front with Alice Camden, owner of and reporter for the Holiday Junction Journal. Then, just before seven, Kade rushed in and took the empty seat next to her.

"Did I miss anything?" he asked, slipping off his jacket and hanging it on the back of the chair. He'd changed out of his work clothes and was wearing a black Henley that clung a little to his chest and arms. When did Kade get arms?

"Vi?" His voice jerked her out of the daze apparently caused by Kade's recent acquisition of biceps.

"Huh?" she said.

"I asked if I've missed anything."

"Oh!" She shook her head. "No, they haven't even started yet."

"Okay, good." He shoved up his sleeves and sat back, one leg propped on the opposite knee.

"What are you even doing here?" she asked. "This doesn't seem like your kind of thing."

"I can't believe you would say that," he said, affronted. "I *care* about this town, Vi."

She glanced pointedly at the snack table, laden with cookies and cupcakes. "I think you *care* about Mrs. Patterson's baked goods."

Kade, to his credit, didn't miss a beat. "Supporting local merchants is the responsibility of every Holiday Junc-tian, Violet."

"Junc-tian?"

"Junction-ian?" Kade crinkled his brow, considering.

A gavel pounding drew their attention to the front of the room, where Mayor Kendricks stood at a wooden podium. "The meeting will come to order!" he shouted over the various conversations.

Joshua Kendricks had been the mayor of Holiday Junction for as long as Vi could remember. She figured he must have been in his sixties by now, his once blond hair was now white, but still slicked back with an abundance of pomade, his skull shining between the lines made by his comb. Tall and skinny, he was full of awkward angles and pointy joints. When she was little, Vi used to wonder if his knees and elbows would be sharp if she touched them. He wore gray trousers and a knitted cardigan over his white shirt, buttoned to his chin. His wife had died before Vi was born, and the mayor dedicated his life to his work. He owned the local real estate brokerage

—and, as mayor, he took Holiday Junction very, very seriously.

Vi thought that was probably why he was still in office. He annoyed a lot of people with his zealous pursuit of making HJ the *number one tourist destination on the West coast. Who cares about Disneyland?* But he was dedicated to the town, and they knew he would never do anything that would hurt it, or them.

"I said come to order!" Mayor Kendricks pounded the gavel one more time, and the room fell into silence. "Thank you," he said, setting the gavel down. "I've called this meeting to address several urgent issues at hand—" He looked up as the door opened and Liam walked through. "Thank you for joining us, Mr. Durant."

If there was one thing you could count on, it was that the mayor would shame you if you were late for a meeting.

"Sorry, Joshua," he replied, finding a seat across the aisle a few rows up from Vi. He looked back at her and smiled as he took off his jacket.

Her stomach flipped, and she smiled back. Kade sighed heavily beside her.

"What?" she asked him.

"Shhh . . ." he said, pressing a finger to his lips, his eyes laser-focused on the man at the podium.

"As I was saying," Mayor Kendricks drew attention back to himself. "Replacing the stop sign at 3rd and Rockport with a stoplight—" A chorus of groans overwhelmed him.

"What's all that about?" Vi whispered to Kade.

"He wants to have a light installed in front of his office," he whispered back. "He's been trying for almost a year, but nobody will back him on it."

"—expert testimony in support of the idea!" The mayor pounded the gavel until the room quieted. "Boomer, come on up here." He waved a blocky man with a comb over toward the podium.

"Boomer Benedict is an expert witness?" Vi asked. He'd been a few years ahead of them in school. A star linebacker, but not the sharpest knife in the drawer.

"He does work in Joshua's office," Kade explained. "I tend to think he may be a bit biased."

Boomer stood at the podium next to Joshua, who apparently was smart enough not to ask the man to speak freely.

"Boomer, tell the people what happened the other day," Joshua said, waving a hand toward the audience.

Boomer looked at him blankly. Joshua rolled his

eyes. "In the crosswalk . . . at lunchtime . . ." He leaned in and hissed. "With Jerome?"

"Ohhh." Boomer nodded, finally understanding. "Jerome hit me with his car."

Jerome Standish, owner of the insurance office next to Joshua's brokerage, shot to his feet. "I did no such thing!"

Joshua slammed the gavel on the podium. "Boomer, you were crossing the street, right?"

"Yep." He nodded.

"On the corner of 3rd and Rockport . . . coming back to the office after lunch?"

"Yep."

"And the defendant's car—"

"I'm *not* a defendant." Jerome was still standing and threw up his hands. "I didn't hit him!"

"—came out of nowhere and hit you, is that right?" the mayor asked.

"Banged my knee up good," Boomer said with a nod.

"Which just goes to show," Mayor Kendricks said smugly, "that a stoplight is desperately needed on that busy street corner."

Kade snorted. "Like *any* street corners around here are busy."

"Now wait a minute," Jerome shouted over the

mumbling crowd. "I should get to speak in my own defense."

"This is not a court of law," Joshua said, waving a hand dismissively. "We should vote on the light."

"Oh, let the man speak," Liam called out, and a few others agreed loudly.

"Fine, fine, then." The gavel sounded again. "Jerome, what do you have to say?"

"Thank you." Jerome straightened, and raised his right hand. "I solemnly swear—"

"Not a court of law," Joshua said again, releasing an annoyed breath. "Please just say what you've got to say."

"Oh, okay," Jerome said. "It's true I was in my car on that day. I was eating a sandwich. I like to listen to audio books on my lunch hour and my headphones are on the fritz, so—"

"What kind of sandwich?" Alice, the *Journal* reporter asked.

"What does that matter?" Joshua asked in exasperation.

"I need a complete report," she replied, sniffing haughtily.

The mayor said nothing but motioned for Jerome to respond.

"Uh, meatloaf," he said. "And barbecue potato chips. And one of Anne's brownies for dessert."

The crowd murmured in approval, and Mayor Kendricks looked like he was about to have an aneurysm.

"Yes, yes, the brownies are wonderful. Now, can we please get on with it?" he prompted.

"Right." Jerome nodded. "Anyway, I was eating and I saw Boomer coming across the street, and then there was this bird—"

"Oh yeeeaah." Boomer nodded slowly. "I forgot about the bird."

"It flew right into him and he was waving his hands and screaming—"

"I wasn't *screaming*—"

"And he wasn't looking where he was going and ran right into the front of my car."

"What kind of bird?" Alice asked, scribbling wildly in her notepad.

"It was a really big bird," Boomer said, holding his hands about a foot apart.

"A crow?" she asked.

He frowned. "No, bigger than a crow."

"Looked like a hawk to me," Jerome offered. "Maybe an owl."

"It doesn't matter what kind of bird it was!" Joshua shouted.

"It matters to me!" Jerome said, affronted. "Got a big dent in the front quarter panel. Gonna cost me five hundred bucks to fix it!" Jerome folded his arms, frowning at Boomer. "I wasn't going to make a big deal about it, but if Boomer's going to accuse me of hitting him—"

"No!" Boomer held up his hands. "It was an accident. Jerome didn't hit me. I ran into him!"

"That's better," Jerome said with a defiant nod. He sat down and Mayor Kendricks wearily rubbed his hands over his face.

"Given these developments, I think it best to table the topic of a new stoplight at 3rd and Rockport until the next meeting," he said.

"Second!" Jerome shouted out.

"All in favor?" All hands shot up. "Opposed?" Nothing.

"Motion passes. The issue is tabled," Joshua said grumpily.

"And this," Kade whispered to Vi, "is why I come to town meetings."

Vi suppressed a giggle and eyed the cupcakes.

It was good to be home.

Six

Kade hadn't realized how much he'd missed hearing Vi laugh. He hadn't really thought about it back then, but now—

Well, turns out he'd missed a lot of things about Vi. Go figure.

He could see her out of the corner of his eye, watching Joshua lead the town meeting, discussing the route for the Cupid 10K on Valentine's Day. He wasn't sure why. The route was the same every year. But Joshua was nothing if not thorough, and he supposed that was what made him a good mayor.

Vi shifted next to him, and her thigh pressed against his for the briefest second. His breath caught.

"Sorry," she murmured, pulling away and crossing her legs.

"No problem," he rasped.

She glanced at him. "Are you getting sick?"

Kade shook his head, eyes focused straight ahead. These weird responses to Vi were getting out of hand. It was almost like he was seventeen again, and he had not liked being seventeen. All those hormones raging out of control. It was not a good look for him.

"And you'll all be happy to know," Joshua said with a victorious smile, "that the new hearts for the lamp posts will be delivered next week. Decorating can continue per the schedule. We will just move the hearts to the end, so everyone's happy,"

There was a brief smattering of applause.

"Which leads us to the decoration competition between local merchants," he said, consulting the agenda before him. "Judging will commence the week before Valentine's Day, and the judges are, as usual, anonymous."

He flipped a page. "I feel it necessary to remind you all to keep the decorations tasteful. No naked Cupids—I'm looking at you, Nora. And no shirtless men. This is Holiday Junction—"

"Not Las Vegas!" everyone shouted in unison. It was a familiar refrain, where the mayor was concerned.

"All right then," Joshua said, "that leads us to the Sweetheart Ball. Anne, where do we stand?"

Anne Patterson got to her feet, adjusting her glasses. "Well, we've hit a bit of a glitch," she said. "As you've all heard, Naomi's mom is sick, and she had to go back east. And Ellie Anderson went into early labor, so we're a bit shorthanded on the planning committee. Would anyone like to volunteer?" She glanced at Lou, who nodded slightly.

Well, that was weird.

The room fell into silence, which was also weird. The townspeople of Holiday Junction were always ready to volunteer for anything.

Joshua looked out sternly over the audience. "Come on, people, it's time to pull together in this time of need—"

Vi snorted. "Sounds like a national emergency."

"It kind of is," Kade whispered. "Be ready for the telethon. Save the Sweetheart Ball."

Vi smirked.

"We're not leaving here until we have some volunteers to help these ladies out," Joshua said.

He saw Lou elbow Vi, and the two had a quiet conversation. Finally, Violet's shoulders fell and she raised a hand. "I can help."

Joshua smiled widely. "Good, good. Thank you, Vi. I'm certain your Broadway experience will help make this a memorable event."

Vi opened her mouth, and Kade was sure she was going to reiterate that she'd never actually been on Broadway, but apparently, she thought better of it. "Thanks," she said. "I'll do my best."

Lou grinned at Anne, who winked back.

"We could use one more, at least," she said. "Someone who could do a little heavy lifting?"

This time, there was no wait for a response. Liam Durant raised his hand. "I'm in," he said.

"You, Durant?" Joshua looked surprised.

Liam shrugged. "Sure. I have the time. And it's for the good of the town." He smiled over at Vi, who smiled back.

And Kade . . . he didn't like that one bit.

Without another thought, his own hand shot up. "I want to help, too," he said.

"Excellent!" Joshua looked like the cat that got the cream. "I have full confidence in your team, Anne. I'm sure the Ball will be the best yet."

Anne smiled widely. "I'm sure it will be, too. Thank you, everyone."

At that point, Mayor Kendricks adjourned the meeting and everyone descended on the treats table. Kade sat, stunned, unsure of what had just happened.

Liam approached them, offering a cupcake to Vi. She thanked him and licked the buttercream frosting.

"Looks like we'll all be working together," Liam said, his gaze focused on Vi.

"Looks like it," Vi said, breaking apart her cupcake so she could make it into a sandwich, the frosting in the middle.

"Anne told me there's a meeting Thursday afternoon," he said. "And we're still on for dinner Friday, right?"

Dinner? He glanced sideways at Vi, wondering why she hadn't mentioned that.

"Absolutely," she replied, a blush crawling up her neck. "I'm looking forward to it."

Liam grinned. "Me, too."

Kade's own cookie tasted like dust in his mouth. He took a sip of coffee. So this was happening. Vi-and-Liam Version Two.

Great.

"Well, I should go," Liam said. "I'll see you at the meeting Thursday."

"See you."

Kade straightened and stepped in front of Vi a little. "Yeah, see you Thursday," he said. He held Liam's gaze, and why did it feel like a challenge?

Liam didn't seem to feel it, though. He smiled at Kade. "Yeah, man. It'll be fun," he said. "Like old times." He said goodbye and walked away.

Vi turned on him. “You're acting kind of weird. What was that all about?” she asked.

Kade shrugged and said nothing. Because, in reality, he had absolutely no idea.

On Wednesday afternoon, Kade had been uncharacteristically quiet on the drive home. Vi tried to initiate conversation a couple of times, but after several halfhearted, one-word answers, she gave up. When they pulled into the driveway, he looked over at her, almost seeming surprised that she was in the passenger seat.

“I'll come over in a few and prune those trees for Lou,” he said.

“Oh, okay. Thanks.”

He nodded and got out of the car and headed inside without looking back. With a confused sigh, Vi went inside herself. She couldn't figure out what was going on with Kade. He almost seemed mad at her for some reason, although she had no idea what she could have done. She set up at the kitchen table to correct some papers and got lost in theater terms for a half an hour, until Kade's knock at the front door brought her back to the question at hand.

There was no point in guessing. She might as well just ask. Kade was one of her oldest and closest friends, after all. If he was upset with her, she couldn't make it right until she knew why. She stalked to the front door and threw it open, a surprised Kade standing with his fist poised to knock again.

"Hi," he said.

"Are you mad at me?" Vi demanded.

"What? No!" he stammered. "Why would you think I was mad at you?"

"Oh, I don't know," she replied, unconvinced. "You've been all quiet and weird since the meeting last night."

Kade seemed genuinely surprised. "I haven't been weird," he said. "I just have some things on my mind."

"What kind of things?" she prodded.

He arched a brow at her. "*Private* things."

She perched her fists on her hips. "Since when do we have *private* things?"

"Oh, I don't know," he replied. "Since when do you have dates with Liam and not tell me?"

That stopped Vi in her tracks. "Well, since when are my dating habits your business?" she asked defensively.

"They're not!"

"Well then . . ."

"So, if that's not my business, then why are the private things on my mind *your* business?" He waved one hand with a flourish, the other holding a set of pruning shears.

"Well . . . I guess they're not—"

"Right."

But Vi didn't like that. At all. What was he hiding?

"I have a date with Liam Friday night. He's taking me to dinner," she said, waiting expectantly.

"That's nice." He brushed by her and headed to the back door.

"Wait!" She closed the front door and rushed to catch up with him. "I've shared my thing, now you share your thing."

"My thing?" He scrunched up his nose at her, playing confused.

She stomped her foot. "Come on, Kade. You know how it drives me crazy not to know things!"

"Did you just stomp your foot at me?"

"Yes!" She stomped it again. "Tell me!"

Kade finally snorted out a laugh, shaking his head. "You haven't changed a bit."

"Tell meeeee," she pleaded, pulling on his arm.

"Kaaaadddeeee . . . telll . . . meeeee . . ." "All right. All right," he said, and she grinned, knowing she had won.

She always won.

He walked out back and looked up at the tree, deciding where to start.

"Kaaaaade . . ."

"Okay!" He laughed, snipping off a long spindly branch. "There's not much to tell," he said. "There was someone I thought I might be interested in—"

"Really? Who?"

"—but I don't think it's going to go anywhere." He cut off another branch. "She's . . . dating someone else."

"Oh." Vi felt bad for Kade, she did. But she also felt something . . . else. Something she couldn't quite put her finger on. Or didn't want to. A tight and dark feeling in the pit of her stomach.

"Sorry," she said.

He shrugged. "No big deal."

Kade kept cutting off the dead branches and Vi grabbed a wheelbarrow and piled them in. They worked in silence for a while, but there was still some tension in the air. Vi wasn't sure exactly what it was—Kade didn't seem upset, really. More resigned, if she had to put a word to it.

"Are you sure you're okay?" she asked, unable to let it go.

Kade dropped the pruners and helped her pile the branches into the wheelbarrow. "I'm fine. I've been friendzoned. It's not the end of the world." He grabbed the wheelbarrow handles and hoisted it up. "It's not the first time, and I'm sure it won't be the last."

And that surprised Violet. In all the time she'd known Kade, she'd never known him to really like a girl. Even in high school, he had casual dates, but nothing serious. And she'd never known him to be interested in someone who wasn't interested in him right back.

She stood by the tree and watched him dump the branches in a pile next to the back fence. It must have happened while she'd been gone, she surmised. Violet felt a rush of possessive anger come over her. How could someone not see how amazing Kade was? What a great boyfriend he would be?

Kade opened the shed in the back corner of the yard and emerged after a few minutes with a hammer and a couple of boards. He waved her over to a section of fence with two broken pieces and handed the wood to her as he used the hammer to remove the damaged boards.

"Can you hold that right there?" he asked, moving the wood into position with his hands over hers. His palms were broad and calloused and . . . big. When did his hands get so big? Violet couldn't understand how Kade seemed to have grown over the past decade. She didn't think that was possible. Didn't people stop growing after they graduated from high school?

But Kade was tall, his frame dwarfing hers as he bent over her, adjusting the position of the fence board.

Vi felt her skin warm, a rush of heat filling her cheeks. She swallowed. Maybe she was coming down with something.

Kade didn't seem to notice. He pulled a couple nails out of his pocket and hammered the board into place, then did the same with the second one. He stood back and studied their work.

"That should hold, I think," he said with a nod.

Violet still felt a little unsteady, but she agreed. "Thanks for coming over. And doing this. I—" She turned to face him, and he was suddenly so close. She could see the flecks of gold in his brown eyes . . . the spot on his cheek where he missed shaving this morning.

She cleared her throat. Why were her hands shaking?

"Thanks for being there for my mom, all these years," she said. "You didn't have to—"

Kade waved it off. "It was no problem."

"I know," Vi said. "I know you think it's no big deal, but it is. To me. It means a lot to me that you've been looking out for her. So, you know . . . thanks." She looked up at him, her heart pounding in her chest. Vi felt herself leaning forward on her toes, and was he moving closer, too? Her breath caught and she licked her lips.

Kade's eyes flicked down, and for just a moment she thought—

She thought maybe—

His gaze locked on hers and she froze in place, unable to move. Unable to breathe.

Then Kade shook his head a little, coughed, and stepped back, looking away as he rubbed the back of his neck.

"So," he said. "Is there anything else that needs to be done?"

Vi blinked, her brow creasing. "What?"

He pointed the hammer around the yard in a wide arc. "Anything else that I need to fix while I'm out here?"

"Oh!" Vi stepped back, smoothing her hair back, her fingers trembling. "No, I don't think so. Mom hasn't mentioned anything."

"Okay, then." Kade gave her a small smile, then walked over to the shed to put the hammer away.

Vi watched him go, stunned. What in the world had just happened? Had she—had she been ready to kiss Kade?

She shook her head. That was insane. Kade was her friend. One of her best friends. They'd grown up together. He was almost like family.

And he definitely didn't think of Violet like that. She puffed her cheeks and blew out a breath. He was hung up on someone else, anyway.

What was she thinking?

Kade came out of the shed and locked it before heading her way.

She was just lonely. After everything with Ben, the slightest hint of kindness had her ready to throw herself at her oldest friend. She was so grateful that he hadn't seemed to have noticed, or if he did, he didn't say anything.

"I better head home." Kade slipped his hands into his jean pockets. "I have a huge pile of tests to grade."

Vi made a face. "Sounds like fun." She followed

him to the front door and opened it for him. "See you tomorrow," she said.

"Bright and early," he agreed with a wink.

Kade jogged down the steps and headed next door. Vi closed the door and watched him through the front window, frowning when he headed toward the sidewalk, instead of into his own house. He waved at a woman walking toward him, and Vi recognized her as Lena McKenna. The woman was all smiles as she spoke with Kade, and Vi could hear laughter, even though she couldn't make out what they were saying.

She watched them interact, a light bulb slowly glowing over her head.

Could Lena be who Kade had been talking about? The one he was interested in?

Finally, Kade turned and headed up his own front steps, still smiling, while Lena approached Vi's. Violet stepped back from the window, embarrassed that they might catch her watching.

Lena knocked on the door and Vi counted to three before opening it.

"Lena, hi!" She put on a wide smile and pulled her friend in for a hug.

"I had the afternoon off, so I thought we could

get started on all that catching up," Lena said. "If you're not too busy?"

"No, no. I have some stuff to grade, but I have plenty of time," Vi replied. "Come on in."

Lena hung her coat by the door and followed Vi into the kitchen, accepting a glass of iced tea as they sat at the breakfast bar.

"So, how's everything going?" Lena asked, stirring some sugar into her tea. "Are you getting into the groove at school?"

"I think so?" Vi replied. "I mean, it's only been a few days, but I think it's going well. After the first day, I wasn't sure I could do it—"

"You?" Lena laughed. "Of course you can do it!"

"Well, thanks for the vote of confidence, but teenagers can be tough, you know?"

"I'm well aware," Lena said, taking a sip of her tea. "What's happened to the youth of today? We were nothing like that."

"Oh no," Vi said somberly. "We were pillars of virtue."

"Highly responsible."

"Extremely mature."

"Oh!" Lena bounced on her seat a little. "Remember junior year when we snuck into the boys' locker room and put Vaseline on all the toilet seats?"

"See?" Vi held up her glass. "Extremely mature." They clinked glasses and burst out laughing.

They chatted for a while, filling each other in on what they'd been doing since high school. Lena shared stories about her travels overseas, and Vi had some interesting stories of her own about life in New York.

"It's weird to think I was there while you were," Lena said. "I spent about a week in New York before I left for Europe. We might have passed each other on the street and never known it."

"It's a big city," Vi agreed.

Lena leaned in and bumped her shoulder with her own. "I'm glad you're back."

Vi smiled. "Actually, so am I," she said. "I didn't think I'd ever say that."

"HJ gets under your skin," Lena said, nodding. "You think you can leave it behind, but it drags you kicking and screaming right back in." She mimed pulling a rope to emphasize her words and Vi laughed.

She eyed Lena sideways as her friend chewed on a piece of ice. "I saw you talking to Kade, earlier," she said, and then she felt foolish. Why was she bringing this up?

"Hmm?" Lena looked at her blankly for a moment. "Oh, yeah. We were just talking about the town meeting." She shook her head. "Bet you missed Joshua."

"Oh yeah," Vi said. "He's a trip." She jiggled the ice in her glass, unsure how to proceed. "So, what do you think of Kade?"

"What do I think of him?"

"Yeah, I mean . . ." Vi tried to search for the right words. "He's a good guy, right?"

"Of course," Lena replied. "Kade's great."

She fought back a surge of frustration. "I mean, he'd make a good boyfriend, don't you think?"

Lena studied her for a moment. "Sure," she said slowly.

"I agree!" Now she was getting somewhere. "Can you believe that he was telling me he might be interested in someone . . . but they were interested in someone else?"

Lena frowned. "That's too bad."

"I know!" Vi said, slapping a hand on the counter.

Lena chewed on her lip, her eyes narrowing. "Did Kade mention *who* he was interested in?"

Vi leaned in. "Not by name, but I think I have an idea."

"Oh really?" Lena looked pleased.

"Mm hmm," she sat back. "And let's just say I think Kade may be mistaken. Do you think I'm right?"

Lena looked confused for a moment. "Well, wouldn't you know—"

The front door slammed, cutting off their conversation as Lou blew into the kitchen. "What a day!" she exclaimed, pouring herself a glass of tea. "I had a whole box of special orders go missing, and let me tell you, the customers don't want to wait. The postal service needs to get its ducks in a row, or it's small business owners like me who'll suffer." She took a drink of tea and looked from one of them to the other.

"Hi, Lena, how've you been?"

"Fine, Lou. Just catching up with Vi." She took her glass over to the sink and dumped the ice. "I really should be going, though," she said. "It's getting late."

Vi trailed after her to the front door. "You'll think about what we talked about, right?"

"What we talked about?" She looked confused. Why was she confused? Lena needed to learn to keep up if she was going to be dating Kade.

"About Kade," Vi prompted.

"Oh, right." Lena nodded. "Don't worry. I'm sure everything will work out," she said, reaching out to run a hand down Vi's upper arm.

Well, that was a weird response.

"Okay," Vi said, the word stretching out.

"Come by the shop sometime," Lena said, putting on her coat. "I'll buy you a scoop and we can figure out what to do about it."

"About what?"

Lena rolled her eyes. "About Kade, obviously."

"Oh, okay." Vi was feeling a little lost.

"Bye," Lena said, before calling back to the kitchen. "Bye, Lou!"

Vi's mom returned the sentiment and Lena left, quickly walking down the street.

Violet closed the door and made her way back into the kitchen.

"That Lena's such a sweet girl," Lou said as she got out the makings for spaghetti.

Vi grabbed the big pot and filled it with water. "She is. She's perfect for Kade."

Lou dropped the can of tomato sauce and it rolled under the counter. "For Kade?"

Vi nodded, turning off the water and putting the pot on the stove. "He's got a crush on her, but he thinks she's not interested."

"He does?"

"But I think she's *very* interested." She adjusted the heat on the stove, then got down on her hands and knees to retrieve the tomato sauce.

"She is?"

She got up and handed the can to her mother. "I think they'd make a cute couple, don't you?"

Lou seemed genuinely confused. "I suppose." She shook her head. "You're telling me Kade told you he's interested in Lena?"

"Well, not in so many words," Vi admitted. "He just told me he's interested in *someone,* but thinks she's interested in someone else. But I figured it out."

Lou huffed a laugh. "Oh," she said, and why was she smirking? "You figured it out, did you?"

"It's not so hard if you have good instincts," Vi said with a smug grin.

"You don't say."

"So, everything's going to work out fine." Vi went to the fridge and took out the makings for a salad. "Who knows? Maybe he and Lena will double date with Liam and me."

It made perfect sense. Two of her closest friends together. It was a wonderful idea. Right?

Vi stared out the window at the newly repaired fence. That almost kiss—if that's what it even was—could have been a huge mistake. She would have completely freaked Kade out. And the last thing she wanted to do was get in the way of his happiness with Lena.

Right. It was a wonderful idea. They'd be perfect for each other.

So why did she feel so hollow?

"Vi, are you okay?" Lou asked quietly.

She turned to find her mother watching her with concern etched on her features.

"Me? Of course!" She forced a smile. "Everything's great!"

And it would be. Like Lena said, everything was going to work out just fine.

Seven

They met at *Chalmers Chapters* Thursday evening to discuss the Sweetheart Ball, gathering around the large table in the back used for book club meetings and other special gatherings. Vi was the last to arrive, since she had rehearsal after school and had walked to the shop again. Kade had offered to wait for her, but the day was dry and Vi didn't mind walking.

Plus, she still felt a little weird about what had happened in her mom's backyard. Not to mention the whole Lena situation. Vi didn't know how she felt about all of that, to be honest. She wanted Kade to be happy, obviously. And Lena was a wonderful person. They'd make a great couple.

But why did that thought put a sour feeling in her stomach?

She could hear them all talking as she made her way past the bookshelves to the back of the store, and took a deep breath, blowing it out slowly before she stepped around the corner and into their sights. Lou,

Mandy, and Anne sat along one side of the table, Kade and Liam on the other, with an empty spot between them.

"There you are!" Lou said, waving her in. "You're just in time. We were about to talk about the decorations."

"Sorry I'm a little late," she replied. "Rehearsal went long."

She spotted a plate of sandwiches and her stomach rumbled. "Are those chicken salad?"

Kade slid the platter toward her and shoved the chair on the end out with his foot. "They're calling your name."

Vi grabbed a napkin and sandwich and was just about to sit down when she realized that Liam was watching her. She paused, mid-sit, then oh-so-gracefully stood back up and walked behind Kade to take the seat between him and Liam, across from her mother.

Between her best friend, and the guy she was dating. Ish.

Finally settled, she took a huge bite of her sandwich, only to look up and find all three women watching her.

She chewed. Swallowed. And finally asked, "What?"

"Nothing!" Lou said, suddenly interested in the notebook before her.

Liam poured her a cup of water and handed it over. "We were just discussing the merits of twinkle lights versus paper lanterns."

"Oh yeah?" She took a sip. "Which side are you on?"

He smiled. "I think twinkle lights are a classic choice."

She smirked. "Bold stance."

Kade snorted, and Vi swiveled around to look at him. "I take it you disagree?'

"I was just saying it might be nice to try something new." He spread his large hands out on the table before him. "We have twinkle lights for everything. We have twinkle lights in the streets. We've never done paper lanterns. Ever."

Liam took in a deep breath. "That's because paper lanterns are for funerals, not for Valentine's Day."

"Says who?" Kade asked.

"There's a reason we always use twinkle lights," Liam said slowly, as if speaking to a child. "Everyone loves twinkle lights."

"Well, maybe everyone might like to try something new," Kade said, just as slowly. "Maybe they haven't seen how nice paper lanterns can be. Maybe they need to give them a shot."

Violet felt like she was watching a tennis match. A very odd tennis match with lighting options instead of yellow balls.

"There's something to be said for the classics," Liam said through a gritted-teeth smile. "Twinkle lights and Holiday Junction. They have a history. They belong together."

Wait. What? Vi was getting more confused by the moment.

"Well, maybe it's time for Holiday Junction to try something else," Kade said, his voice getting louder. "Maybe twinkle lights have had their chance and it's time for a change!"

"Holiday Junction doesn't want a change!"

"Gentlemen—" Lou said, clearing her throat, but they didn't seem to hear her.

"How do you know what Holiday Junction wants?"

"I think it's pretty obvious."

"Well, I would disagree—"

"Gentlemen—"

"—and you would be wrong!"

"Gentlemen!" Lou shouted, slapping a hand on the table. "If you don't mind!"

Both men opened their mouth as if to respond, but at Lou's glare, they snapped them shut and sat back, silently fuming.

What in the world was that all about? Violet looked from one to the other, but they wouldn't meet her eyes. She shrugged and took another bite of her sandwich.

"All right," Anne said, brown eyes wide. "I think there's room at the ball for twinkle lights *and* paper lanterns. Kade's right—there's nothing that says we can't try something a little different."

Kade preened. He literally preened. Vi hadn't seen someone do that before, but there was definitely some preening going on.

And she thought she might have heard Liam mutter something under his breath, but she wasn't entirely sure.

"So, someone will need to drive into the city on Saturday to pick up the smoke machine and some decorations we've already ordered." Anne checked something off on a piece of paper, then looked up. "Vi, are you up for it?"

The question took her by surprise, but she shrugged. "Sure. I'll have to borrow my mom's car—"

"Oh, I don't know," Lou said, frowning. "I kind of need my car on Saturday."

"You do?" Vi asked. "What for?"

"I have some things to do," she said vaguely.

"I can drive," Liam offered. "Vi might need some help with the heavy lifting anyway, right?" He smiled at her. "It'll be fun."

Her skin heated. Why did his smile always have that effect on her?

She played it cool, though. "Yeah, sure," she said. "It'll be fun."

"Oh, but I was hoping to get Vi's help with the music," Mandy said, shuffling through her own pile of papers as she pulled a pencil from the pile of braids atop her head. "With her musical background she's the perfect choice."

"What exactly do you need?" Vi asked, setting down the remnants of her sandwich and wiping her hands on a napkin.

"The D.J. is coming by tomorrow afternoon to go over the playlist," she replied. "It's the only time he's available, but I can't do it. Friday afternoons are so busy at the shop."

Vi consulted her phone. "I'm pretty open tomorrow afternoon. I'd be happy to meet with him if you fill me in on what you're looking for."

"I can help," Kade said quickly. "I mean, I've

been there for the past decade of Sweetheart Balls. I can probably offer some assistance music wise."

"Perfect," Mandy said, and Vi thought she shot Anne a kind of smug smile, which didn't make any sense at all.

Her mom's friends were weird.

The meeting wrapped up pretty quickly after that. They ran through responsibilities for refreshments, (Vi wasn't tagged for that, thank goodness) discussed ticket sales, (at a record high, much to Lou's glee) and the last-minute promotional push, which, as far as Vi could tell, involved posters and flyers, as well as an upcoming spot in the Journal. To be honest, she was kind of daydreaming through that part of the meeting. Liam had leaned forward, his elbow on the table, chin on his hand, and that made his cologne waft her way a little bit.

It was very distracting.

Finally, Lou declared the meeting adjourned, and Vi headed out of the store, flanked by Kade and Liam.

"Mom, you coming?" She turned back when she saw Lou wasn't following them.

"You go on ahead," she replied. "I need to talk to Anne and Mandy for a bit."

"I can give you a ride," Liam offered at the same

time as Kade said, "Ready to go?" motioning toward the door.

"Oh!" She looked from one to the other, finally settling on Liam.

"I'll catch a ride with Kade," she said. "He's right next door, and I hate to have you go all the way across town."

"It's no problem—" Liam began, only to be cut off by Kade saying, "Great! Let's go."

He opened the door for Vi, then followed her out, letting the door swing shut on Liam.

"Hey!"

"Oh, didn't see you there," Kade said. "Sorry, dude."

Sorry, dude? Since when did Kade talk like a surfer? And he really didn't seem all that sorry.

"No worries," Liam replied, although Vi could tell he was irritated.

She wasn't sure what was wrong with Kade, but he seemed to be mad at Liam for some unknown reason.

Vi tried to smooth things over a bit, turning to Liam. "We're still on for dinner tomorrow night, right?"

"Absolutely." He grinned at her, his white teeth and sparkling eyes making her knees feel like jello.

"I'm looking forward to it." He reached for her hand and the touch made her skin tingle.

"Me, too," she said breathily.

He leaned in, shooting a glance toward Kade before pressing his lips lightly to her cheek. She could feel the blush heating her face, and bit her lip, looking up at him.

"I'll see you tomorrow night," he said.

"Okay," she replied, watching him walk away toward his car.

"Can we go now?" Kade asked flatly.

Vi jumped a little. She'd almost forgotten he was there.

"Yes, we can go now," she said, mimicking his grumpy voice. "What's your problem, anyway?"

They got into the car and Kade started the engine. "I don't have a problem."

"Right," Vi drew the word out. "So, you are really just that passionate about paper lanterns?"

He pulled away from the curb, his face darkening as he spotted Liam waving before he got into his own car.

"I don't know. That guy gets under my skin, lately," he said gruffly. "He acts like he's the expert on everything."

"I don't think that's tru—"

"I mean, yes, he's a big, fancy lawyer, but success isn't only about having a good job and a lot of money, you know?"

"I know that," Vi replied. "There's more to Liam than his job."

"Oh yeah?" Kade shot her a glance, then checked both ways before turning the corner. "Like what?"

She shifted to face him. "What's this all about, Kade?"

His jaw tightened, then he took a deep breath and let it out, slowly. "It seems to me that you're living in the past."

Vi gaped at him. "What?"

"Come on," he scoffed. "You're living in your old room, going out with your high school boyfriend—"

"That's—that's—" she sputtered.

"Are you so desperate to re-live the glory days—"

"*Desperate*?" Her hands began to shake. How dare he? "Who are you calling desperate?"

He pulled into the driveway and slammed the car into park. "I'm just saying—"

"You're just saying that I'm a pathetic has-been who hasn't moved past high school?" she all but screeched. "Is that what you're just saying?"

"Vi—" he groaned.

"No, don't you *Vi* me," she spat, anger rearing up

like a lion. "You have no idea what I've been through. No idea."

"I know that Ben—"

"You know *nothing* about Ben." She unbuckled her seatbelt and reached for the door handle, shocked to find herself fighting back tears. "And apparently you know nothing about me, either!"

"Vi!"

She got out of the car and slammed the door before stalking toward her house.

"Vi, come back. Let's talk about this."

"I don't want to talk to you!" she shouted over her shoulder. "And don't worry about giving me a ride tomorrow. I'll call an Uber!"

"We don't have Uber!"

She ignored him and ran up the steps and through the front door, slamming it behind her. Frustration and anger welled up in her and she breathed deeply, unwilling to give in to the tears.

No more tears.

Squaring her shoulders, she walked into the bathroom and splashed some water on her face, then drank from her cupped hands. She was under control. She didn't have to think about it. No more tears.

She looked at herself in the mirror and frowned,

remembering what Kade had said. Was she just trying to re-live some glowy memory of high school she clung to like a pathetic loser? Was she so messed up after Ben—

She choked on a surge of emotion, her hand going instinctively to her stomach. Vi clutched at her sweater and closed her eyes, willing her control to return. After a few minutes, she opened her eyes, but didn't look at the mirror again before leaving the bathroom.

Vi didn't want to think about it. She didn't want to think about any of it. And if there was something she'd gotten pretty good at over the past six months, it was not thinking about things.

Instead, she retrieved her bag and pulled out her lesson plan book, and a stack of papers to grade. She had work to do. And she had to figure out a way to get to work tomorrow.

Maybe she could get a ride with her mother. It'd mean Lou would have to get up early—which she wasn't a huge fan of—but she'd probably help her out this once. If not, she could always walk.

Violet bent over her work and put aside all thoughts of Kade and Liam . . . and Ben.

Late that night, when Vi was almost asleep, she heard the distinctive sound of a guitar outside. Chords first, then a gentle, rhythmic picking.

"What in the world?" she murmured.

She got out of bed and went to the window, pulling back the curtain so she could peek outside. She couldn't see much. Her window faced the side of Kade's house, his own childhood bedroom window across the small stretch of lawn. Many nights they'd stayed awake late, whispering across to each other and hoping they wouldn't get caught.

Kade didn't sleep there anymore, of course. He was on the other side of the house, in his parents' old room. She wondered if that was weird for him. If it brought back painful memories. They'd been killed in a car accident not long after Kade graduated from college. Vi had wept when she heard, and called Kade to tell him how sorry she was. She'd gotten his voice mail, and only now did she realize that was the last time she'd called him.

Vi caught a flash of movement near the front of the house and realized Kade was on the front porch. Quietly, she cracked the window so she could hear him play a little better.

It took her a moment to recognize the tune. Even then, she wasn't certain she did.

Until he started to sing.

I'm sorry. I'm so, so, so sorry

I acted like a tool

I'm sorry. I'm so, so, so sorry

For being such a fool

Vi giggled. It was a song they'd made up when they were ten or eleven. A way for them to apologize to each other without having to actually apologize.

It had seemed like a good idea at the time.

Like the guy who broke the Atari

Or the one who crashed the Ferrari

Who puked when he ate calamari

Who fed the lions bread on safari

I'm so, so, so,

Vi quietly sang along.

so, so, so

so, so, so

She snorted, trying not to laugh out loud.

so, so, so

I'm so, so, so, so, so, so . . . sorry.

He finished with a last rattly strum and peeked out from under the porch roof. She couldn't see his face in the darkness, but knew he was waiting for her to say something.

"You did act like a tool," she said.

"I know." He set the guitar down, leaning it against the porch rail. "Can we talk?"

It was late, but Vi knew they needed to do this. "I'll be down in a minute."

She put on slippers and an old, knitted cardigan, wrapping it around herself over her pajamas as she tiptoed down the stairs. She made her way outside and over to Kade's front porch. He was standing next to the porch swing, watching her nervously.

"You could get arrested for disturbing the peace," she said by way of greeting.

His lips twitched. "I know a lawyer."

She snorted. "After today, Liam would probably let you rot in jail."

Kade sighed heavily and motioned toward the swing. "You want to sit?"

Vi shrugged, still not completely willing to let him off the hook, but she finally sat next to him on the swing. He pushed it with his foot, the chain squeaking overhead.

"I really am sorry," he said after a few minutes.

Vi nodded, looking out over the front yard. "It's okay."

"Thanks."

"But I have to know," she said. "What was that all about? Is it Liam? Is it me?"

"No, it's not—" He ran his hands through his hair, then dropped them in his lap. "It's not either of you. I had a bad day and overreacted."

"Really," she said flatly. "You're going with *I had a bad day*?"

He huffed, his lips quirking up. "You never did let me get away with anything."

"That's my job as your friend," she pointed out.

"Right." Kade nodded. "I guess—I guess I missed you, when you were gone," he said after a bit of a pause. "And I like having you around again."

She leaned in to bump his shoulder with her own. "I like being around."

"And I guess," he said slowly, "the thought of you and Liam picking things up where you left off—"

"We're not *picking things up*," she said, throwing her hands up in frustration. "It's just dinner!"

Kade eyed her skeptically. "Believe me. Liam wants to pick things up. He wants to pick all the things up."

Vi rolled her eyes, unwilling to argue the point.

"Anyway," Kade continued, "I might have felt a little jealous, thinking he was going to be taking up all your time. Maybe. A little bit."

"Maybe," she said.

"A little bit."

Vi wasn't sure if she wanted to laugh or cry in relief. She hated being mad at Kade, but now . . . after the song. And the confession? How could she stay angry?

She nudged him again. "You're dumb."

He smirked. "*You're* dumb."

"Look," she said, turning to face him and tucking a foot under her. "You're my friend. That's not going to change. Liam or no Liam."

He sighed. "I know."

"And I'm not some starry-eyed teenager who's going to get lost in her boyfriend's life, you know? I'm an independent woman!"

"Right." He nodded emphatically.

"I am!"

"I know you are!"

"I lived in New York!" she said. "I rode the subway! I ate street meat!"

Kade made a face. "Gross."

Vi wasn't going to let it go until she knew he understood. "The point is, no matter what happens with Liam, I'm not going to abandon you." She ducked down to look in his eyes. "Not again."

"Vi—"

"No, I want to say this." She touched his arm.

"I'm sorry. I'm sorry I left and didn't keep in touch. I shouldn't have done that."

He shrugged a shoulder. "It's okay."

"It's not, but—" She pressed her lips together, then sang. "*I'm so, so, so, so, so, so sorry!*"

Kade laughed. "I'm sorry, too."

"I can't believe you sang the song."

"Hey, that's an amazing song," he protested. "One of my better pieces, if I do say so myself."

"Well, you didn't write it alone," she pointed out.

"Ah yes," Kade said, nodding. "You wrote the *so, so, so, so, so, so* part."

She held up a finger. "And I believe the calamari line was mine."

"It was not!"

"Was so!"

They both burst out laughing and Vi found herself leaning into him, happy that they'd made amends. The swing creaked as it swayed back and forth, their breath puffing out in clouds of steam.

"You know you can talk to me, right?" Kade said quietly. "About Liam. About . . . anything."

Ben. She knew what he meant.

"I know," she said. They swung for a little while longer before she said, "I guess you were right, in a way. I was happy in high school. So happy. And maybe I do regret what happened with Liam." She sat up and turned toward him. "Is that so wrong? To want to see if we still have something? *Could* still have something?"

Kade studied her face, then shook his head. "No, of course not," he said. "You should do whatever makes you happy. If that's Liam, then I'll support you a hundred percent."

"Thanks."

"Even if he's kind of boring."

"He's not boring!"

But Kade was smiling, so she knew he wasn't serious. And she wasn't really mad.

"I guess things were just simpler back then," she said quietly, looking out over the yard again. "We were young and the world was wide open, you know? We didn't know disappointment, not really. We didn't know—" Her throat closed up and she swallowed thickly.

"Are you okay?" he asked.

"Not really," she admitted, glancing at him. "But I'm getting there."

"Do you want to talk about it?"

Vi considered it. Thought about telling Kade everything. But she felt peaceful and safe sitting next to him on that old porch swing, and she didn't want to ruin it.

"Not right now," she said, looping her arm through his and leaning her head on his shoulder. "Maybe later?"

"Okay."

"Right now, I'd just like to sit here and swing for a while, if that's all right?"

"That's perfectly fine." He kissed the top of her head. "I'm always up for a late-night swing."

And for a few precious moments, they sat there in silence, watching the world go by.

Eight

The next afternoon, Kade and Vi waited at the high school for the Sweetheart Ball D.J. to show up. It was after three on a Friday, so the school was empty, and they stood at the front doors, watching the parking lot for his car.

Kade hid a yawn behind his fist. He was tired after their late night, but relieved that things seemed to be back to normal between them. He felt a little foolish for how he'd acted, but Vi seemed to be over it, so he tried to be, too.

It was absurd for him to be jealous of Liam. Sure, he might become Vi's boyfriend—again—but Kade was her closest friend. He always had been, and always would be.

That was all he needed. Right?

"Do you know this guy?" Vi asked.

"No, he's new," Kade replied. "I guess the regular guy was already booked or something."

Vi hummed in acknowledgement and shoved the door open. "I think that's him."

A middle-aged man in a trench coat approached, carrying a briefcase.

"That's him?" Kade mused.

The man spotted them and waved, quickening his steps. Under the coat he wore a pinstriped suit with a pristine white shirt and a red tie. His dark hair was neatly combed, gray at the temples, and a pair of round, wire-rimmed glasses perched on his nose.

He looked more like a politician or an accountant than a D.J.

"Hello, I'm David," he said, shaking their hands. "You must be Kade and Violet, yes?" He had a slight European accent, although Kade couldn't quite place it beyond that.

"Yes," Vi replied. "Thanks for coming."

"Of course, of course." He waved a hand dismissively. "You need me to come. I come."

They led him down the hall to the choir room and sat around her desk. David put his briefcase on his lap and flipped it open, withdrawing a file folder, a hot pink MP3 player, and a matching portable speaker. He set it all on the desk, pushing aside her stapler and phone to make room.

Over his head, Kade widened his eyes at Vi, who pressed her lips together, trying not to smile.

"So," she said. "We were discussing possible themes—"

"Oh, I know the perfect theme," David said, spreading his fingers in jazz hands. "Disco Retro Glam Funk."

Kade stifled a snort. "Disco Retro . . ."

"—Glam Funk," David finished with a firm nod.

"Umm . . ." Vi shot a confused look at Kade. "I'm sorry, but what exactly is that?"

He looked at her like she could very well have been an idiot. "DRGF is all the rage," he said. "All the best parties are doing it." David picked up the MP3 player, pressed a button, and an electronic beat pounded out of the speakers. He began to shift his neck from side to side in time with the beat, pointing his finger up to accentuate the high-pitched melody weaving into the bass.

"You see?" he said over the music. "It's catchy, yes?" The music stopped abruptly, and he froze, then it kicked in again, and he resumed the neck-shifting and finger-pointing, adding a shoulder roll every now and then.

Kade couldn't believe what he was seeing. What he was hearing. He tried to catch Vi's eye, but she was staring at the D.J., mesmerized.

"It's very nice," Vi began, but David had his eyes closed, lost in the music, and didn't hear her.

"It's very nice!" she said, louder, and David startled, his eyes flying open.

"Would you mind turning it off?" she asked. When he did, she smiled.

"I'm sure Retro Disco—"

"Disco Retro," he corrected.

"Right." Her smile grew a little stiff, and Kade really, really had to try not to laugh.

"It's . . . it's great," she said, feigning enthusiasm. "But I think we were hoping for something a little more . . ." She looked toward Kade, obviously asking for help.

"Traditional?" he offered. "Classics, maybe?"

"Yes!" Vi said, snapping her fingers and pointing at him. "That's it. Classics. Frank Sinatra. Etta James."

"But more modern stuff, too," Kade added.

"Right," Vi said. "The key is romance. That's the theme. It's Valentine's Day, after all." She gave David a hopeful smile, but he looked at her blankly.

"Classics," he said.

"Yes."

"Romance." He sniffed.

"Yes."

"Sinatra." He got a sour look on his face.

"Well, not only Sinatra," Kade said. "Sam Cooke, The Beatles, Aretha Franklin . . . Adele?"

David considered them both, distaste still evident on his features. "Yes, well. I suppose that's another way to go. If you wish."

Violet smiled, and Kade knew she was trying to be charming. "We wish, I think?" She glanced at Kade. "Yes, we definitely wish."

"Very well," David replied, with another sniff. "You are the boss, after all."

He flipped through the file folder and pulled out a single sheet of paper. He perused it briefly, then handed it to Violet. "Romance classics," he said.

Violet took the paper and laid it on the desk so Kade could see it, too. It was a list of songs, and as Kade reviewed it, he realized it was exactly what they were looking for.

"This is perfect," he said.

"Of course it is," David replied, packing up his MP3 player. "It's relatively easy to be common."

Vi mouthed *common?* at Kade when David wasn't looking. He chewed on the inside of his cheek to keep from laughing.

David snapped his briefcase shut. "Very well, now that we have established the playlist, there's the matter of the deposit." He arched a brow expectantly.

"Oh, of course." Vi pulled a check out of her purse and handed it to him. He scrutinized it, then folded it neatly in half and slid it into his jacket pocket.

"Do you need anything else from us?" she asked.

"No," David stood and buttoned his suit jacket. "Unless you'd like to alter the song list at all?" He gave her a hopeful look, and Violet squirmed.

She was tempted to say yes. Kade could tell. She wanted to tell David to go ahead and throw in some Retro Disco tunes for the fun of it.

He decided to save her. "I think the playlist is great, as is."

"You're certain?" David asked. "You don't find it a bit . . . dull?" He scrunched up his nose in distaste.

"Well, Holiday Junction is a rather traditional town," Kade said, with what he hoped came across as sympathy. "People don't push a lot of boundaries."

David frowned. "Their loss," he said shortly. Then he picked up his briefcase and walked out of the room.

"Umm . . . thank you?" Violet hurried to the door, calling out after him.

He raised a hand in acknowledgment. "I'll be at

the venue at three p.m. on the fourteenth," he said. He turned the corner and was gone.

Vi turned back around, her eyes wide. "What in the world was that?"

"I have no idea," Kade replied. "I was kind of pulling for the Retro Disco Glam Funk."

Vi snorted. "Disco Retro."

"Right." Kade started to shift his neck and point his finger like David. "I don't know. It was definitely catchy." He made a *boom-ch boom-ch* sound, imitating the electronic beat and got up, shaking his hips.

"You need to stop that right now," Vi said, laughing. "You look ridiculous!"

"*Boom-ch boom-ch* I don't know *boom-ch* what *boom-ch* you're talking about." He danced around the room, swiveling his hips and shimmying his shoulders. "It's all the rage!"

He shimmied over to Violet, still making the electronic music sound. "Come on, don't be *common*!"

She laughed and started to dance with him, rolling her fists over each other, then pointing in a wide arc from one side of the room to the other before switching hands to go the other direction.

"That's it," Kade encouraged. "Now you're Glam

Funky!" He grabbed her hand and lifted it to spin her under his arm, then pulled her close, shifting to walk across the room, tango-style.

They laughed and pivoted to go back the other way, then he dipped her low over his arm and she shrieked.

"Don't drop me!"

"Who me?" He jerked his arms, just a little, and she screamed again, clinging to him.

He pulled her back up and her arms settled over his shoulders as she laughed, trying to catch her breath. Her blue eyes sparkled, her cheeks flushed pink. Kade could feel the warmth of her hands on the back of his neck and his own breath caught.

She looked up at him, smiling, and he couldn't move. Couldn't think. Couldn't look away.

Violet blinked, her smile falling. "Kade? Are you okay?"

"What?"

Violet stepped back, and he jolted, letting her go abruptly. "Sorry," he said, forcing a smile. "Got a cramp."

She grinned at him. "Must be tough to be so old."

"Hey! I'm only two months older than you!"

Vi shook her head sadly. "But those two months make all the difference."

He pulled her into a headlock and rubbed his knuckles lightly into her hair, making her squawk.

"Say it!"

"No!" She squirmed and pushed but couldn't get away.

He rubbed a little harder. "Say. It."

"Kade is the King and I am but his lowly servant!" She shoved at him and he finally released her.

"Thank you," he said smugly.

Vi straightened her hair. "One of these days I'm going to make *you* say it."

He slipped on his jacket and threw an arm over her shoulders. "But that day is not today."

She rolled her eyes. "Come on. Let's go home."

And why did that sentence send a rush of heat through him?

They headed out to the parking lot and got into the car. Kade chewed on his lip, eyeing her sideways.

"So, are you excited about tonight?" he asked.

"Tonight?" she asked, looking out the window, distracted.

"Your date with Liam?" he prodded.

"Oh!" She turned to face him. "Yeah, I am. It'll be nice to catch up." She picked at a thread on her jeans, opening her mouth a couple of times, then snapping it shut.

"What is it?" Kade asked on a huff.

She inhaled deeply. "Last night, you . . ."

"Yes?"

She shook her head. "You said you thought Liam was definitely interested in me."

"Well, I think the fact that he asked you to dinner would show you that," he replied.

"Maybe." She pulled at the thread again.

And he hated that she seemed so uncertain. So uneasy.

"He's definitely interested," Kade said finally. "He's got stars in his eyes every time he looks at you."

She looked up at him, blushing. "You think?"

"Yes!" He gave her an exasperated look. "How many times do you want me to say it?"

She shrugged, but when she looked out the window, she was smiling. Obviously, he'd told her what she wanted to hear. Liam and Violet were great together. They always had been. He'd make her happy, and all Kade wanted was for Violet to be happy.

As he turned the corner and headed home, he tried to convince himself that was true.

He almost . . . *almost* succeeded.

That evening, Vi stood in front of the bathroom mirror, frowning at her reflection. Lou watched from the doorway as she walked out and back into her own room to change into the yellow dress.

Again.

"You need to make up your mind. He'll be here any second," Lou warned.

Violet didn't know why she was so nervous. She knew Liam. Probably better than anybody.

Or at least she used to.

That thought stopped her in her tracks. What if he'd changed? What if he wasn't sweet and nice and smart anymore? What if he was—

"Vi?" Lou's voice snapped her out of her rabbit hole of panic. "He just pulled into the driveway."

Violet let out an unladylike grunt and faltered for a moment, one dress half-pulled off, the other half-pulled on. In the end, she went with the yellow, flowered dress, even though it was kind of summery and it was February. Liam had always liked her in yellow.

She tugged on a matching cardigan and slipped on her shoes, rushing to the bathroom as she heard her mom open the front door. Vi checked her lip gloss, then her teeth, smoothed her hair, and took a deep breath.

Here we go.

She forced herself to walk slowly—casually—down the stairs, only to almost trip when she spotted Liam standing at the door, tall and handsome in a dark suit and yellow tie. He grinned at her, blue eyes twinkling.

"Well, you two have fun," Lou said, backing toward the kitchen. "Remember your curfew!"

"Mom!" And she was seventeen once again.

Lou laughed and Vi could hear her getting something out of the fridge. She turned back to Liam.

"You look nice," she said.

He took her hand and spun her once. "You look amazing. Pretty as a picture."

"Thanks." She blushed and touched his tie. "We match."

He smiled down at her, still holding her other hand, and her stomach flipped. "Guess we're in sync," he said.

"Or you're stalking me," she said, arching a brow.

Liam's eyes widened. "I would never!" Then he seemed to realize she was joking. He laughed. "Oh. Right . . . well, shall we?" He helped her on with her coat and opened the door for her, following her out to his car and opening that one, too.

"I could get used to all this gentleman stuff," she said, glancing toward Kade's house. She thought she saw the curtain twitch in the living room, but she was probably mistaken.

"You deserve it," Liam replied, before closing the passenger door and rounding the front of the car to get in his own seat. "Ready?"

"Ready."

They drove to a new restaurant on the edge of town that used to be a dilapidated sawmill when Vi last saw it. The broken wood siding had been replaced, the weeds cleared out of the creek, and the water wheel turned slowly, dumping buckets full of water as it rotated.

"I can't believe what they've done here," she said, looking up at the building and the gold painted sign reading The Mill, hanging over the glass front doors. "It's so beautiful."

"Wait until you see the inside," he said, leading her forward with a hand on her lower back. The touch made her shiver . . . made her nervous, maybe . . . and she swallowed thickly.

He held the door for her again, and she almost gasped out loud when she walked in. The old sawmill was definitely gone, replaced by a beautiful dining room with gleaming hardwood floors, thick beams overhead, and large black-framed windows looking out over the water wheel and the winding river heading to the south. A second-floor lofted area ran along three walls, with wrought iron railings allowing diners to look down onto the main floor. But the central feature was a floor-to-ceiling stone fireplace in the middle of the room. Arched openings on three sides revealed the dancing flames, and there were comfortable-looking leather chairs and benches placed around the fireplace where some customers were enjoying drinks, Vi assumed, while waiting for a table.

"Who did this?" she whispered half to herself.

"Some chef out of L.A.," Liam replied as they approached the hostess station. "Moved here about a year and a half ago and opened The Mill last fall."

"Well, they did an amazing job," Vi said. "I wouldn't have even recognized it. Hey—" She leaned toward him, lowering her voice. "Remember when we used to sneak out here senior year?" she asked, flushing at the memory.

He winked at her. "How could I forget?"

The sawmill had been a premiere make-out spot back then. Young couples would pick their way through the building, which was supposed to be haunted, although Vi wondered if it was the teenage boys of Holiday Junction who started that rumor in the first place in an effort to get their girlfriends to hold their hands just a little tighter.

Anyway, looking back, it was pretty dangerous—the mill was practically falling down, and they ignored the warning signs posted by the county. But in its own way, it was also romantic. And there were many evenings she and Liam spent in his car, overlooking the river, talking and kissing and being teenagers.

Liam touched her back again and she was jolted out of the memory. She smiled at him as they followed the hostess to a table near the window by the water wheel. Vi watched it slowly spin as she took her seat and slipped out of her coat.

"I can take that for you," the hostess offered, and she hung them both on hooks along the far wall.

"This is so much nicer than the place we used to go," Vi teased.

Liam smiled. "Well, attorney-at-law pays a little better than football player and part-time fast food server."

Vi laughed and opened her menu. She opted for a sea bass dish with grilled cherry tomatoes and Liam ordered a steak. He ordered a bottle of wine and they sipped it and chatted while they waited for their meal.

"So, tell me everything," he said, spreading butter on a piece of sourdough bread.

"Everything?" She laughed. "I think you'll need to be a little more specific."

He took a bite of the bread and nodded, swallowing. "All right then, tell me about New York. Did you love it?"

Of course, New York made her think of Ben, but she pushed those thoughts aside. Ben had no place here.

"I did," she replied, swirling her wine. "It's so big and noisy, but there are also these little communities that you don't really get to know unless you live there. The people in my building, the business owners on my block–There was this little old lady who ran a convenience store near my apartment. She always threw in a day old doughnut when I'd go in for coffee."

Liam made a face.

"It was sweet!" she protested. "And it tasted pretty good if you dunked it."

"I'm sorry, but that's disgusting," he said with a laugh.

"Well, when you're broke, you'll eat pretty much anything," she said, her smile falling slightly.

Liam reached across the table and placed his hand on hers. "I'm sorry. I didn't mean—"

"No, no, it's all right." She pulled her hand back and waved it dismissively. "It's no big deal." She took another sip of her wine. "Anyway, I worked so many odd jobs I lost count—waitressing, barista, all the typical side jobs for an actress. Went on a lot of auditions. Got a few parts. Lost a lot more. And I ended up here, right back where I started."

She sat back and rubbed her finger idly around the base of her wine glass. "It sounds so depressing when I say it out loud."

"Why do you say that?" Liam asked. "You had a dream. You went after it. Maybe it didn't work out quite how you hoped—"

Vi snorted. "That's putting it mildly."

"—but you're still using your gifts to make the world a better place," he said, nodding firmly.

She fiddled with her earring, scrutinizing his face. "You make it sound so noble."

"Teaching is noble," he replied. "And it's not easy, I know that." Liam's mom had taught history at the high school until she retired. She'd taught Vi, and all of her friends, at one point or another.

"No, it's not," Vi said, looking out at the water wheel again. "It's just not how I saw my life turning out, you know?"

"You thought you'd be a star," he said, and there was no mocking edge to his voice. "We all did."

She tilted her head, studying him. "You did, too?"

Liam sighed and smoothed his napkin over his lap. "Of course. You were so—" He searched for a word and evidently couldn't find it, so he shrugged.

"I thought we'd go to college. You'd become a big star. I'd become a lawyer—"

"Two out of three ain't bad," Vi muttered.

"Then I thought we'd get married," he admitted. "Eventually. And have a family."

And didn't that make Violet feel like the scum on the bottom of her shoe. "I'm sorry," she said. "For how I—" She shook her head. "I hurt you and it was wrong. I feel terrible about it and I'm so sorry."

Liam gave her a small smile. "It was a long time ago. I got over it."

"I know . . . I'm sure you did." Vi bowed her head for a moment, the guilt still eating at her. Then she looked up. "But I need you to know I am sorry."

"It's okay." Liam looked up as the waitress approached and set their plates before them.

"I tell you what," he said. "If you want to make it up to me, let me try one of those tomatoes."

Vi laughed and held out her plate. He plucked off one of the blistered tomatoes and popped it into his mouth, humming appreciatively.

Vi took a bite herself and had to agree. The meal was simple, but delicious, and they fell into an easy conversation about lighter topics. Liam told her a few stories about college and law school . . . filled her in on what some of their old friends were up to. In return, Vi told him about some of the stranger auditions she'd been on.

"There was one," she said, setting down her fork. "It was for a soap—"

"You auditioned for a soap?" His mouth twisted.

"Hey, don't judge. A job is a job."

His eyes crinkled. "My mistake. Please continue." He sliced off a piece of steak.

"Anyway," she said, "the whole audition was me emoting to the camera. They didn't want me to say a word. I was just supposed to look at the camera and be angry! Be frustrated! Be conniving!"

Liam wiped his mouth and set his napkin on the table. "Okay, I have to see this. Be conniving."

"No!" She laughed, covering her face with a hand.

"Come on. I want to see it. Show me your talent!"

"Okay, okay . . ." Vi forced down giggles, closed her eyes, and took a deep breath.

"Is that it?" Liam asked.

"No!" Her eyes flew open. "I'm centering myself to get into character."

Liam's lips twitched. "Oh, sorry."

"If you don't want to see it—"

"No, no! I do. I promise, I'll be quiet." He mimed zipping his lips and Vi fought back another giggle.

She was a professional, after all.

Vi closed her eyes again and took a breath, then opened them and did her best conniving—an evil smile, arched eyebrow and hands rubbing together gleefully.

Liam burst out laughing. "I have to say that is the best conniving I've ever seen."

Vi did a little bow at the table. "Thank you. That'll be twenty bucks."

"What?"

She leaned forward, eyeing him seriously. "You don't think I perform for free, do you?"

He shrugged and reached for his wallet, but she waved him off, laughing.

"That one's on the house," she said. "Besides, you're driving tomorrow, so we'll call it a wash."

Liam laughed, and Vi felt a sudden rush of relief. She had been so nervous about tonight, but it was turning out fine. Liam hadn't changed. He was exactly the same—handsome, smart, kind. Being with him was like going back in time, in a way. They had so many shared experiences, common memories, and being with him was comforting because of that.

As they shared a piece of decadent chocolate cake, Vi made a decision. She and Liam were right for each other, she was sure of it. And Violet was going to do whatever it took to make sure he knew it, too.

Nine

Kade couldn't sit still Friday night. He felt fidgety and anxious and couldn't figure out why.

He tried to correct papers, but his mind kept wandering. He got up to get something to eat, but nothing sounded good. He flipped on the TV but couldn't find anything interesting. He walked from room to room, not even bothering to turn on the lights, lost in thought.

Kade sighed as he looked out the living room window for the hundredth time, his gaze drifting to the driveway next door.

Again.

What was wrong with him? Ever since the meeting with Vi that afternoon, he'd been on edge. As a matter of fact, now that he thought about it, it'd been longer than that.

Ever since he first spotted her in the driveway, and she'd yanked that suitcase out of the car, her clothes scattering everywhere.

With a huff of frustration, he grabbed his jacket and keys and headed out to the car. He couldn't stand waiting around for Vi to get home from her date—there was no pretending that wasn't exactly what he was doing. So, he'd go for a drive and try to get his mind off things, maybe stop for coffee or ice cream.

In the end, he just drove around town aimlessly, his eye catching on every SUV that looked like Liam Durant's. Was that them at the diner? No, he would have taken her somewhere nicer. Maybe *The Mill* or even somewhere in the city.

In the end, he parked in front of McKenna's, annoyed with himself for acting like a crazy stalker. There was only about a half an hour before the shop closed, and it was empty except for Lena, elbows on the counter as she played on her phone. The perfect spot for Kade to drown his sorrows in a hot fudge sundae.

"Hey!" Lena said, straightening. "How's it going?" She arched her neck, looking behind him. "Where's Vi?"

"We're not joined at the hip," he groused.

"Ouch, okay." She held up her hands. "Didn't mean to poke a nerve."

Kade sighed heavily, rubbing the back of his neck. "You didn't. Sorry. Just a little tired, I guess."

"Mmm hmm," she said, nodding slowly. "What can I get you?"

He got up onto a barstool and tapped his fingers on the counter. "Hot fudge sundae. Double scoop of chocolate peanut butter. Extra whipped cream, please."

Lena scooped the ice cream silently, topping it with a good dose of hot fudge, and squirted whipped cream until he nodded that it was enough. She slid it across the counter to him, along with a napkin and spoon. "Want to talk about it?" She wiped down the counter, waiting.

He shrugged. "Nothing to talk about." He took a bite of the sundae and nodded. "That's the ticket."

"Good?"

Kade took another bite. "Awesome."

Lena didn't press him to talk. It wasn't her style. Instead, she worked quietly, cleaning up dishes and polishing the glasses. Still, it only took a few minutes for Kade to buckle.

"She's out with Liam," he said, licking his spoon.

"What?" She paused, holding her rag in mid-air. "Who?"

"Vi," he said. "She's out on a date with Liam."

"Why?"

"Why?" he huffed out a laugh. "Why do you think, why? Because they're perfect for each other, obviously." He stabbed at his ice cream and took an extra-large bite, wincing at the brain freeze.

"But—" She tossed the rag in the sink. "I thought she and you . . ."

His brow lifted. "She and me . . ." He gestured for her to continue.

"You know." She propped her fists on her hips. "I thought you and Vi finally figured things out."

He studied her carefully. "Figured what out, exactly?"

Lena rolled her eyes. "That *you* are perfect for each other, obviously," she said, mimicking his tone.

He laughed. "Right." He scooped up the rest of the melted ice cream in the bottom of his bowl. "Vi's head over heels for Liam."

"But that doesn't make any—She told me—" Lena stammered.

"What did she tell you?" he asked.

She shook her head. "Maybe I misunderstood," she said, leaning her elbows on the counter, her brow creased. "So . . . she's dating Liam? Again?"

"Go figure, right?" he muttered. "Welcome back to high school."

"And you haven't told her?"

He eyed her sideways. "Told her what?"

"That you're crazy about her!"

"Don't be dumb. We're friends." He shoved the empty bowl toward Lena. "I just want her to be happy."

"Huh," she said, taking the bowl and heading over to the sink.

"What's that supposed to mean?"

"Nothing," she said airily.

"Lena . . ."

"Kade . . ."

He scoffed. "Oh, real mature."

Lena wiped her hands on a towel and turned to face him. "All I'm saying is it's obvious to anyone with eyes that you have more-than-best-friends feelings about Violet Chalmers. You always have."

He opened his mouth to argue, but Lena's eyebrows shot up in challenge, and he opted for another route.

"Okay, maybe that was true in high school, but I got over it," he said. When she kept staring at him, he huffed. "I did! And now—" Now what? He thought he had this all figured out, but now Lena had him questioning himself.

"Look, even if that was true—and I'm not saying

it is," he said, holding up a finger. "It doesn't matter. I'm Vi's friend. She'll always see me as her friend. Nothing more."

"I'm not sure that's—"

"It's the way it is," Kade said firmly. "She's out on a date with Liam. He's who she wants. There's nothing more to say about it."

He got up from the stool and reached for his wallet. "I should let you close up. Here—" He tossed a few bills onto the counter. "Keep the change."

"Thanks." She picked up the money and put it in her pocket. "But Kade, can I say just one more thing?"

He fought the urge to sigh dramatically, but he waved for her to continue.

Lena swiped an errant strand of hair out of her face. "You have a lot of opinions about what Violet wants. What she thinks. But I wonder—have you ever actually *asked* her?"

"That's—"

She held up a hand to stop him from speaking. "You spent a good part of high school pining over that girl, and she never had the slightest idea. I'm pretty sure she still doesn't." Lena leaned forward onto the counter. "If you let that happen again, it's all on you."

"But Liam—"

"She's gone on one date with Liam," she said. "One date. That's hardly a committed relationship."

Kade didn't respond, so she rounded the counter and faced him, putting her hands on his shoulders. "It's not too late yet. But if you don't man up, it might be soon." She smacked his shoulders once. "Think about it?"

Kade nodded. "Okay. Maybe."

"That's all I ask." She grabbed the towel and started wiping down tables. "Now get out of here so I can go home, okay?"

"Yeah. Thanks." He shot her a wave and walked out to his car, his head spinning.

Did he have feelings for Vi? Feelings more than a friend? And if he did—which he was beginning to admit he did—what in the world was he going to do about it?

Saturday morning, Lou sat on a stool in the kitchen, sipping a cup of coffee. Vi was upstairs getting ready to drive to the city with Liam, and Lou felt a bit . . . ambivalent about it.

It wasn't that she didn't like Liam. She did. She

always had. And when she saw him with Vi, they did seem like a lovely couple.

But—

But then she'd see Vi with Kade, and she began to wonder if maybe there might be a better choice.

Lou sighed. Sometimes this matchmaking stuff was stressful.

She got up at a knock on the door and crossed the living room, sipping her coffee.

"Can you get that, Mom?" Vi called from upstairs. "I need a few more minutes."

Lou opened the door, surprised to find Kade standing on the front porch, his hands in his pockets as he shifted nervously on his feet. "Hey, Lou. Is Vi around?"

Well, this could get interesting.

"She's upstairs getting dressed," Lou replied, stepping back. "Come on in. You want some coffee?"

"Um." He licked his lips and shot a glance toward the stairs. "Sure. Coffee'd be great. Thanks."

He took a seat at the breakfast bar as Lou poured him a cup and waved off her offer of cream and sugar. She handed it to him and took a seat next to him.

"So, how are things?" she asked.

"Things are good." Kade spun his cup around on the counter slowly. "How are things with you?"

"Oh, fine," she said. "Anne and Mandy are coming by. We may go to brunch at *The Mill.*"

"Sounds nice."

"It's a great place," she said, watching him carefully. "Liam took Vi there last night, you know. She said it was delicious."

She watched as Kade stared into his cup, his jaw clenching. *Interesting.*

"That so," he said flatly.

"Oh yeah, she had the chocolate cake. Have you tried it yet?"

"Can't say that I have."

Was it wrong that she was having fun with this?

"Well, it's delicious," she said. "There's a hazelnut filling and this buttercream that's just— Well, it's incredible."

"I'll have to try it sometime." He gulped the coffee, then winced, sucking in air.

"Are you okay?" she asked, patting his back.

"Fine," he said through gritted teeth. "Hotter than I thought."

She hummed in acknowledgment but said nothing more. She watched him out of the corner of her eye, waiting . . .

5 . . . 4 . . . 3 . . .

Kade cleared his throat, and Lou nearly laughed out loud. She didn't even get to two.

"So, she had a good time?" he asked, not meeting her eyes. "With Liam?"

"What?" Lou paused with her cup at her lips, then set it down. "Oh, yes, she did. I'm sure it was nice for them to get reacquainted."

"Uh huh." He took another sip, a bit more carefully. "Did she—" The doorbell rang, cutting him off.

"That should be Liam now," Lou said with a sunny smile. She walked out to the living room, aware of Kade right behind her. Violet was already coming down the stairs, and they all met at the door.

Lou could swear her life was better than a soap opera.

Vi opened the door, and Liam gave her a bright smile . . . a smile which fell slightly when he spotted Kade.

"Hi!" Vi said, stepping back. "Come on in. I just need to grab a cup of coffee to go. You want one?"

Liam entered and shut the door behind him. "No, thanks. I have some in the car."

Vi nodded and headed back to the kitchen, leaving Liam, Kade, and Lou standing in a loose circle, the men looking anywhere but at each other, tension thick in the air.

"So," Lou said brightly, only to be interrupted again by the doorbell. She laughed. "It's like Grand Central Station around here."

Anne and Mandy were waiting on the porch when she opened the door, and she waved them in, widening her eyes in what she hoped was a significant look.

"What are you—oh!" Mandy stopped in the entry when she spotted Liam and Kade. "You have company." She smiled widely. "Good morning, boys."

"Morning," they both muttered, as Vi returned from the kitchen.

"Well, hi!" she said brightly. "You ladies have big plans?"

"Just brunch," Anne replied. "But I'd much rather hear about *your* plans." She cast a significant glance toward Liam and Kade, and Lou fought the urge to roll her eyes.

Honestly, her friends were so *obvious* sometimes.

"Well, Liam and I are headed to the city to pick up decorations for the ball," Vi said, slipping into her coat. "I'm not sure what Kade's doing here." She wrinkled her nose at him and he stuck out his tongue.

"I've come to sweep Lou off her feet, obviously," Kade said, throwing his arm over Lou's shoulders.

"Eeww!" Vi made a face. "That's my mom you're talking about!"

"Don't be ridiculous," Lou said, laughing as she shoved Kade away. He grinned but stilled when he noticed Vi watching.

"I came by to talk to you about something," Kade said. He flicked a glance toward Liam. "But it can wait."

Vi wrapped a scarf around her neck. "You sure?"

He shrugged. "Yeah. It's nothing urgent."

"Okay." She turned to smile at Liam. "You ready to hit the big city?"

"I am if you are." He opened the door, holding it for her.

"See you all later," Vi said over her shoulder as she walked out of the house. Liam closed the door and Lou could see him following Vi down the front steps through the side window. Then she realized she wasn't the only one watching.

Kade stood turned toward the living room window, a frown on his face.

"Kade, are you all right?" Lou asked.

He startled, then ran his hands through his hair. "Me? Sure, I'm fine." He walked over and reached for the door himself. "I should go. You ladies have a nice brunch." He was out and gone before any of them could respond.

"Well, that was something," Anne said.

They all peered out the window as Liam and Vi drove away, and Kade stopped, watching them go.

Kade's shoulders fell and he slumped off toward home.

"That poor boy," Mandy murmured, shaking her head.

"Must be tough," Anne said. "And Vi has no idea?"

"Not a clue," Lou replied. "The girl is all stars-in-the-eyes about Liam."

"Well, I think he's a good choice," Anne said, walking away from the window. "They seem perfect for each other."

"You have to be kidding!" Mandy faced her, folding her arms. "Kade is a much better choice. Anyone with eyes could see that."

"Well, *Vi* doesn't see it," Anne retorted, eyes flashing behind her glasses. "That boy is deep in the Friend Zone."

"Which is where all good relationships start,"

Mandy said stubbornly. "He just needs to get up the courage to tell her how he feels about her."

"Lou, what do you think?" she asked.

Lou took a sip of coffee, considering. "I'm not sure," she admitted.

"What? You have to see that Kade is the one."

"No, *Liam* is the one," Anne corrected.

"It's not up to us to decide who's the *one*," Lou said, holding up a hand. "That's up to Vi. We made sure she had time with both of them. But what they do with that time is up to them."

"But she can't make that decision if she doesn't have all the information," Mandy pointed out.

Anne snorted. "What information?"

Mandy rolled her eyes. "That Kade is in *love* with her, of course."

Lou noticed Anne didn't argue the point. It was obvious to all of them that Kade loved Vi, even if Vi had no clue. It had been obvious to Lou even when they were both kids. It only took seeing them together for her to realize that those feelings hadn't gone anywhere.

If anything, they were stronger than ever.

"I have to say, I think Mandy's right," Lou said slowly. "Violet should know how Kade feels about her."

Mandy arched a brow. "Are you going to tell her?"

"Me? No!" Lou laughed. "But a little push in the right direction wouldn't hurt."

"What do you have in mind?" Anne asked, fiddling with the end of her ponytail.

"I'm not sure yet," Lou mused. "But I'll come up with something." She straightened, set her coffee cup on a table, and reached for her coat. "Until then, brunch?"

The ladies smiled. "Brunch."

"So, do you know what exactly we're supposed to be picking up today?" Liam asked as he signaled to get on the freeway.

Vi had been surreptitiously studying his profile, so his question took her a bit by surprise. "What?"

He glanced at her with a lopsided grin. "I asked what we're going to pick up today."

"Oh! Oh, right." Vi fumbled in her purse, her cheeks flaming.

"Mom gave me a list," she said. "The smoke machine, of course. And some 3D hearts and garland —" She pressed her lips together. "Paper lanterns."

She could feel Liam jolt. "Really?"

Vi laughed. "No, not really. They ordered them online. I'm messing with you," she said. "What was all that about anyway?"

"I just think twinkle lights are better." He shrugged a shoulder, but his ears started to turn red.

"Mmm hmm . . ." Vi didn't buy it. "Are you mad at Kade about something?"

"Mad?" He shook his head, his lips turned down. "No. Of course not." He shot her a look. "He just gets on my nerves sometimes."

Vi snorted out a laugh. "He gets on *everyone's* nerves sometimes."

"Not yours." His voice was sharp, his eyes focused on the road ahead.

"What's that supposed to mean?"

"Nothing." He sighed heavily. "Sorry. It's just that you and Kade have always—"

When he didn't finish, she asked, "Always what?"

Liam's jaw tightened, and she saw him visibly try to relax. "You've always been . . . close."

"Yeah?" She gathered her hair up, then let it go. "We're friends. We've been friends since we were little kids. You know that."

He glanced at her. "You're sure that's all it is?"

"What?" Vi gaped at him, and Liam flushed. Did he really think—that she—and *Kade*?

"You can't be serious," she said, reaching out to touch his arm. "Kade is my friend. Yes, he's one of my best friends, but that's all." Vi wasn't sure how to feel about the conversation. She felt bad that Liam apparently was threatened by her friendship with Kade, and she wanted to reassure him. But at the same time, she had to admit she was a bit annoyed by his comments. She drew her hand back and tucked it under her leg.

"He *is* important to me, though," she said. "And if we—if there's going to be anything between you and me? You're going to have to be okay with that."

"I am," he said quickly, darting a worried look her way. "I just—I don't know how to say this without sounding like a jerk." He huffed out a humorless laugh.

She touched his arm again. "Go ahead and say it."

He took a deep breath and blew it out slowly. "The thing is, I like you." He glanced at her again, his face pink. "But I don't want to pursue anything if you're not a hundred percent on board."

Vi's stomach swooped and she could feel her own cheeks heating. "I like you, too," she said quietly.

"Yeah?" He grinned.

"Yeah." She rolled her eyes. "But we've only been on one date," she said. "It's still pretty early to be saying anything is a hundred percent."

"I get that," Liam replied, looking over his shoulder to change lanes. "But does that mean you are interested in a second date?" He sounded a little tentative, unsure.

"Of course," Vi said with a laugh. "That's kind of the point of the whole *I like you* thing."

Liam's smile grew dazzling, and Vi had to fight to keep from sighing out loud.

"In that case, would you like to go to the Sweetheart Ball with me?" he asked.

"I'd love to," Vi replied brightly.

"Great!" He reached out and gave her hand a squeeze before putting his back on the steering wheel. "Hey, you know what I was thinking about this morning?"

"What?"

"Remember junior year when we were counselors at fifth grade camp?" he asked.

"Camp Balto!" She threw her head back and laughed. "We had so much fun!"

"We were such bad role models." He ran a hand through his hair. "Remember the snake?"

"Oh!" Vi slapped his arm. "I couldn't believe you did that."

"Eh, it was a harmless garter snake."

"The girls in my cabin didn't know that! Oi, with the screaming!" She threw her hands up.

He smirked. "I was just trying to get you outside so I could sneak a kiss."

"You were?" She laughed. "Well, it worked. None of the girls would go back into the cabin until the snake was gone."

"Unfortunately, they wouldn't leave your side, either," he said. "So my brilliant plan backfired."

"Serves you right," she said, giggling. "It took more than an hour for Kade to catch that snake."

Liam stiffened slightly. "Kade got it?"

"Yeah, he heard the screams and came running. He didn't even take time to put on shoes, so he was limping the whole way. He said . . ." She trailed off when she noticed Liam's frown and cleared her throat. "Anyway, he grabbed it and the girls went back to bed, but they'd squealed at every little creak because they thought the snake was back. So—"

"Well," Liam swallowed. "Sorry about that."

Vi chewed on her lip, feeling the tension, but not wanting to address it directly.

"Remember the junior prom?" she asked instead. "With that horrible band?"

His smile returned, slowly. "They were really bad."

They chatted about old times for the rest of the drive, and the tension seemed to have lifted, but Violet still felt a little uneasy about what Liam had said. He obviously had some issues with Kade, and Vi wasn't sure exactly what to do about that. Liam was a great guy, and she wanted to keep seeing him. But Kade was—

Kade was family. And she didn't think she could date someone who couldn't accept that.

Liam winked at her and took her hand, holding it gently. She smiled in return, hiding the turmoil in her thoughts.

She wasn't sure how to reassure Liam that Kade was no threat. That she had absolutely no interest in him, romantically-speaking.

Because she didn't. No way. The thought was ludicrous.

Her mind drifted to the night they spent on the porch swing, talking. She loved Kade, of course. He was important to her. She trusted him and enjoyed spending time with him.

But anything more?

That afternoon in the choir room at school flashed before her eyes. They'd been goofing around, dancing like lunatics, but then he'd pulled her close, and as she'd looked into his warm brown eyes, a shiver raced down her spine. She was trapped, couldn't move . . . and for one brief moment she thought—

But then the moment had passed, and she was sure she'd imagined it.

Vi shifted and looked out the window at the passing scenery.

No. Kade thought of her as a friend. Anything else was absolutely ridiculous.

Ten

Kade stood, thumbing at his phone, as he waited for Vi outside the rehearsal hall on Monday afternoon. He wasn't really doing anything but didn't feel like talking to anyone. He'd succeeded in avoiding Vi for the rest of the weekend. After the encounter at her house with Liam, he didn't even know how to talk to her.

He sighed and paced down the hall and back again, running a hand through his hair. What had he been thinking? He'd gone to see her Saturday morning to tell her—what? That he thought he was growing *feelings* about her? He felt like an idiot.

"Get it together, Rivera," he muttered, flopping back to lean against the concrete wall.

He and Vi were headed over to the venue for the Sweetheart Ball to look it over and check out the area where they'd set up for the D.J. He wasn't sure exactly why that was necessary, but Lou had been insistent, saying she really wanted to make sure everything was organized and ready to go for

Saturday night. Kade had never been able to say no to Lou, so he'd agreed.

And now . . . well, now he was wishing he'd pretended to have a cold. Or the flu.

Or the plague.

His eyes drifted over to a butcher paper sign taped to the wall advertising Valentine flower sales. Someone had painted a rather realistic-looking Cupid pointing an arrow, with a speech bubble that read, *$1/flower, what a deal! Show your Valentine how you feel!*

"Yeah, easier said than done," Kade muttered. He sauntered over to the sign, looking into the Cupid's wide, blue eyes. "What are you looking at?"

"Hi, Mr. Rivera!"

Kade whirled around to find a girl with a thick black ponytail, wide brown eyes, and braces smiling up at him.

"Oh." He adjusted his bag, hitching it higher up onto his shoulder. "Hi, Lindsey. How's it going?"

"Good!" Her eyes flicked up to the sign and back. "You going to buy some flowers for your girlfriend?"

"Me?" He stepped away from the sign like it was going to bite him. "No! I mean I don't—"

"—because I'm on the committee and I could get

you a deal, if you want," Lindsey said with an exaggerated wink.

His brow crinkled. "Wait a second. Isn't it a fundraiser for the debate team?"

She shrugged. "Eh, a couple bucks won't matter. Not like we're going to Regionals this year anyway."

Kade managed not to laugh. "Well, thanks for the offer, but no. I'm not buying flowers for anyone."

"Really?" She tilted her head at him. "Because I'd think Ms. Chalmers would love it."

"Ms. Chalmers?"

Lindsey nodded. "She's your girlfriend, right?"

"No!" He could feel his face heating. "She's— We're just friends."

"Oh." Lindsey looked genuinely surprised. "Everyone thought—"

At that moment, the door opened and students poured out of the rehearsal hall, chatting loudly and laughing. Vi took up the rear, smiling at one of her students, who was telling her something with a flail of limbs. She spotted Kade and her smile grew.

His heart seemed to thud to a stop.

Vi waved goodbye to her students and walked over to him, slipping on her coat. She was wearing a bright pink sweater that made her skin glow rosy, and her hair was swept up haphazardly, a few blonde strands twisting around her face.

She was . . . absolutely beautiful.

"Hi, sorry to keep you waiting," she said. "Rehearsal went a little long."

Butterflies took flight in Kade's stomach and he swallowed thickly. "No problem," he said, a little choked.

"You okay?" She glanced at the girl next to him. "Hi, Lindsey."

"Hi, Ms. Chalmers." Lindsey, curse her, was watching him with wisdom in her narrowed eyes that far exceeded her years.

Kade cleared his throat. "I'm fine. You ready to go?"

"Yep." She gave her scarf a tug and turned to leave. "Bye, Lindsey."

"Bye, Ms. Chalmers." The girl arched a brow and sing-songed, "Bye, Mr. Rivera."

"Lindsey." He nodded gruffly. Could he fail a student for being exceedingly annoying? Kade was going to check the rule book on that one.

They got into his car and headed toward the venue. Kade tried to act as normally as possible, and it seemed to work, because Vi chatted away about various things—rehearsal, her mom, the kids in her class.

Then, her chatter stopped abruptly, jolting Kade from his thoughts and he looked over to find her studying him closely.

"What?" he asked.

"What's wrong with you?"

"Me? Nothing!"

She shifted in her seat, turning sideways and tucking one leg under her. "I just said my junior choir climbed the walls and screeched like monkeys," she said wryly. "You're lost in your own little world. What's up?"

Okay, so obviously, he wasn't doing as good a job of acting normal as he'd hoped.

"Nothing," he said, turning around a corner. "I was just lost in thought for a minute."

Her eyebrows shot up. "About what?"

"Nothing I want to talk about," he snapped.

"Sorry!" She immediately stiffened, changing position to look out the side window.

And Kade felt like the biggest jerk. He pulled into the parking lot and stopped, then took a deep breath. "Sorry," he said.

Vi shrugged. "It's okay."

"No, it's not. I just—" He scrubbed at his face.

"I'm dealing with some things and I'm not ready to talk about them. To anybody." He watched Vi carefully, hoping that would satisfy her.

She seemed to loosen up a little, her lips lifting a bit. "Okay," she said. "But you know you can talk to me about anything, right?"

Not this.

"Of course."

"I'm on your side. Always." She reached out and squeezed his arm, the touch sending electricity racing through him.

This was bad. So bad.

"I know." He forced a smile.

"I mean, even if it's—you know—women troubles—"

He choked. "What?"

"I'm just saying!" She gestured toward herself with a flourish. "Woman, here. I can probably lend some expertise."

"Okay—It's not—" Kade reached for the door handle with shaking hands. "I'll keep that in mind," he said finally. "Can we go in now?"

Vi shrugged and got out of the car.

The Beavers Lodge on the south end of town was a large, square structure made of concrete and brick. The Fraternal Order of Beavers had long since vacated Holiday Junction—Kade didn't think it existed anywhere anymore—but the building was often used for town functions, since it was the only place with enough space. The town paid to maintain it, and about five years ago did a renovation to bring it into the twenty-first century. Kade unlocked the door with the key Lou had given him and held it for Vi to enter.

The lodge consisted of three meeting rooms at the front of the building, an office that was rarely manned, but contained a desk and phone anyway. And in the back, a spacious ballroom with hardwood floors, sparkling antique chandeliers that had been scavenged when the old McKinley house was demolished, and a wall of floor to ceiling windows looking out over a grassy meadow and the mountain range beyond.

"Wow," Vi breathed, walking into the ballroom and spinning in a circle. "It looks so different. I remember paneling. Lots and lots of paneling."

"Yeah, they remodeled it a few years ago," he replied.

"Mom told me, but I didn't realize—" She approached the windows. "I can't believe they hid this view for so many years."

Kade took in a deep breath and went to stand

next to her. "I know. I guess the Beavers were more concerned about keeping their secret rituals secret."

She side-eyed him. "The Beavers had a lot of secret rituals, did they?"

"Rumor has it," he said, nodding sagely.

Vi turned to face him, crossing her arms. "What kind of rituals?"

"Well, if I told you, they wouldn't be secret, would they?"

Vi laughed, and he smiled. He loved the sound of her laugh. His heartbeat sped up as he watched her. Maybe he was wrong. Maybe he could tell her about his feelings.

Maybe she would understand.

She stepped away and surveyed the room. "I guess we should figure out where to put the D.J."

"Right." He shook his head and joined her, pointing at the wall to the right. "Your mom said the refreshments will be over there—tables scattered on this side of the room, with dancing over here." He pointed to the left.

She nodded, tapping a finger on her lips. "So, what do you think? Right in the middle, or one of the corners?"

"Nobody puts David in a corner," he quipped.

Vi laughed. "Bad movie impression aside, I think

you're right," she replied. "I get the impression David's a bit of a diva."

"I think that's pretty obvious."

She walked across the wood floor, her heels clicking, and her hair glimmering under the light from the chandelier. "So, who are you taking?"

"Hmm?" He blinked, trying to catch up.

"To the ball?" she clarified. "Who are you taking?"

"Oh, I haven't asked anyone. I hadn't even thought about it."

"Really?" She propped her fists on her hips. "Well, you better get on it before it's too late."

Before it's too late . . .

Could this be his chance? Maybe he didn't have to lay out his feelings all over the floor, after all. He could just ask her to the ball. As friends.

Coward.

He licked his lips nervously. "Since you brought it up, I was thinking—"

"How about Lena?" she suggested.

That took him a bit off guard. "Lena? Lena McKenna?"

She rolled her eyes. "How many Lenas do you know?"

"Why would I—"

"Oh!" She clapped her hands together. "We could double. You and Lena and Liam and me! It would be so much fun!"

Liam. A double date with Vi and Liam. Kade's heart sank. He'd pretty much rather be locked in a closet and forced to listen to Disco Retro Glam Funk all night.

"Actually," he said. "I promised your mom and the ladies that I would help out all night. Refreshments, coat check, that kind of thing. So, I won't be taking a date."

"Oh, bummer." Vi pouted, then slapped him on the arm. "Well, that's nice of you. I didn't even think of volunteering." She walked over to the windows and did another little twirl. "You know, I thought I hated Holiday Junction when I left, but there are parts of it—" She glanced back at him. "It kind of grows on you, you know?"

He couldn't keep from asking, "Are you going to miss it, do you think?"

"Miss it?"

"When you go back to New York. Or L.A."

She bit her lip and looked back out the window. "Oh, yeah. I guess I will," she said quietly. Pensive.

"And will you miss Liam?"

Vi turned to face him. "What's this all about? Why are you being so weird?"

"I just think if you're going to be leaving, it's kind of wrong to lead him on," he said, lifting his chin. Where were these words coming from? Because it definitely wasn't his brain.

"I'm not leading Liam on," she said, eyes narrowing. "And honestly, that's none of your business." She went to move past him and Kade grabbed her elbow to stop her.

"You're right," he said, looking into her hurt blue eyes. "I'm sorry. I shouldn't have said that."

She pulled her arm away. "So why did you? What is up with you, Kade?"

And how could he answer that question?

"I don't know," he replied, and it was the truth, to a certain degree. "I've just been feeling weird lately. Maybe I'm getting an early mid-life crisis."

Vi's lips twisted. "You're not even thirty."

He gave an exaggerated eye roll. "That's why they call it an *early* mid-life crisis. Sheesh. Keep up, Chalmers." He draped an arm over her shoulders. "Come on. I hear your mom's making pot roast tonight, and I intend to charm my way to getting some of that." He waggled his eyebrows and Vi laughed.

"You're about as charming *as* a pot roast."

"Hey! I resemble that remark."

Vi groaned as they walked out of the ballroom and Kade tried not to audibly sigh in relief. He'd almost blown it and told Vi everything, but what would have been the point in that? She had no plans to stay in Holiday Junction—and if she did, it wasn't Kade she'd be staying for. She didn't want him as anything but a friend. That much was obvious.

They walked out to the car and Kade laughed in all the right places, teased in all the right places, but inside, he felt cold . . . lost.

He had to get over this, and fast. Because if he didn't, that would mean the only way to protect his heart would be to stay away from Violet Chalmers.

And that was something he knew he couldn't do.

Vi sliced off a bite of tender roast and popped it into her mouth, smirking at Kade, sitting across from her at the table. It hadn't taken much charming at all for him to nab an invitation to stay for dinner. Her mom was a softie. Plus, she loved to see people enjoying her cooking.

Right now, however, she was driving them both

crazy going over preparations for the ball. She ate with her left hand while going down a rather detailed list with her right.

"So, you're sure that's the right place for the booth?" she asked them both. "Because once I have the guys set it up, they won't have time to move it."

Vi met Kade's gaze, and she could tell he was trying not to laugh. "It's the perfect spot, Mom, I promise," Vi said, buttering a roll.

"Okay, then. I'll take your word for it," she murmured, checking off an item on her list. "The caterers will be there around four. You can help with that, right, Kade?"

"Right," he replied through a mouthful of potato.

Another check. "And you can both be there Friday to help with decorations?"

"No rehearsal on Friday, so check that baby off," Vi said, miming a check mark.

Lou gave her a prim look. "You laugh, but my lists have kept Holiday Junction events on track—"

"—for the last twenty years," Vi and Kade said in unison.

Lou frowned, but Vi could see the corners of her mouth twitching. "You are bad children. No dessert for you."

Kade perked up. "There's dessert?"

Lou leaned across the table, her face stern. "Not. For. You."

Kade looked like he was about to cry, and Vi reached across the table to pat his hand. "Don't worry. We can sneak some when she falls asleep."

Lou made an outraged noise and Kade grinned. It was good to see him smiling. Something had really seemed to be on his mind when they were at the lodge, and Vi couldn't figure out what it was. It was weird that he was so upset with her about dating Liam when she planned to leave Holiday Junction eventually. But to accuse her of leading him on?

Was she? The fact was, Vi wasn't all that sure anymore that she wanted to go back to New York. Sure, she missed performing, and the art of it all. But the crowds and the cockroaches and the being broke all the time?

Yeah. That part wasn't so great.

And she'd really been enjoying working with the kids. Teaching them in class and helping them during their rehearsals. It was rewarding in a way she hadn't expected.

Go figure.

She pressed the back of her fork against her last potato, smashing it, then raised it to her mouth to lick it off. Kade was watching her.

"What?" she asked.

"You still do that," he replied.

She swallowed her potato and took a sip of water. "Do what?"

"Eat stuff off the back of your fork." He smashed his own potato, holding it up to demonstrate. "You used to do it with everything—potatoes, carrots, cake."

"I did?" Vi looked at her fork, thoughtful. "I guess I never even realized." But Kade did. And that gave her a warm feeling inside—that someone would know her so well.

But Kade always had, hadn't he?

The doorbell rang and Vi popped up, wiping her mouth. "I'll get it."

When she opened the door, she was surprised to find Liam standing on the other side of it. "Hey!" she said, pulling him into a hug. "What are you doing here?"

"I was in the neighborhood and thought I'd stop in," he said, taking off his coat and hanging it on the hook. He followed her into the dining room. "I thought if you weren't busy we could grab a cup of coffee—" He halted when he spotted everyone around the dining table. "I'm sorry. I'm interrupting dinner. I should have called."

"Oh, don't be silly, Liam, you're always welcome here," Lou said, with a calculating look in her eye that Vi didn't like. "Have a seat. Can I get you a plate?"

Liam pulled out the chair next to Kade and sat down. "No, thank you. I've already eaten."

The room settled down into silence broken only by the scrape of Kade's silverware against his plate. "This roast is amazing, Lou," he said, taking another slice off the platter. "You're a genius in the kitchen."

"Don't try to sweet talk me," Lou said dryly. "I'm not budging on the dessert."

Vi and Kade burst out laughing, quickly joined by Lou, but Liam looked at them all blankly.

"Did I miss something?" he asked.

"Oh, it's nothing," Vi replied. "Just being silly."

Lou wiped her mouth and set her napkin on the table. "Since you're here, Liam—" She consulted her list. "Will you be able to help with decorations on Friday?"

Liam glanced at Vi, who mouthed a *sorry* at him. "Sure," he said. "No problem."

"Excellent. And would you—"

"Liam, didn't you mention coffee?" Vi said brightly, standing up from the table. "We should go get that. Right now. Before they close."

"Oh, okay." Liam got to his feet. "Are you sure—"

"I'm sure," Vi said with a nod. "See you all later!" she called out to her mom and Kade as she pushed Liam toward the front door.

"Mom's driving us crazy with her list," she whispered to Liam as they got their coats. "Believe me, you don't want to be trapped in there."

Liam shot a look back toward the dining room. "What about Kade?"

"Kade's on his own. It's every man for himself," she hissed. "Now go, man. Go!"

They drove into town and Vi took in the now-completed decorations. The controversial hearts sparkled on top of the faux-gas lamp posts, twinkle lights sparkled overhead, and cupids, hearts and flowers adorned every window. It really was beautiful, and Vi could understand why tourists flocked to the town.

Liam pulled to a stop and Vi realized they were parked in front of McKenna's Creamery. "I thought we were going for coffee?" she asked.

"We were, but since you missed dessert, I thought ice cream might be a better choice." He tipped his head. "Is that okay?"

"Yes, sure. It's fine," she replied. "McKenna's is the best."

Liam got out of the car and jogged around to open her door. He took Vi's hand but stopped her when she started to walk toward the shop, and pulled her close.

"What are you doing?" Vi laughed, wrapping her arms around his neck. His big hands spanned her waist as he grinned down at her and Vi's stomach swooped.

He leaned down, his lips brushing hers. "I couldn't wait to do this again," he murmured.

She smiled against his mouth. "Well, don't let me stop you."

Liam kissed her again, and it brought back memories of high school dances and moonlit nights. When he finally pulled back, her knees were weak, and she leaned into him as they turned to walk into McKenna's.

The shop was pretty busy, so they waited in line behind a mom with three kids who couldn't decide what flavor they wanted. Lena was all smiles and patience, but when Vi finally got to the front of the line, her smile fell.

"I'm never having children," she whispered. "What'll it be, Vi?" For the first time, she glanced behind Vi and her smile faltered a bit. "—and Liam? Hi, Liam."

"Lena." He nodded. "Looks like they're keeping you busy tonight." The bell rang over the door and another family came in.

"It's the Monday night special," she replied, jerking a thumb at the sign over her shoulder promoting two-for-one scoops. "Not sure if it's a blessing or a curse."

They got their ice cream and found a small table near the window. Pretty soon, they were once again reminiscing about old times.

"You know," Liam said, dipping a spoon into his bowl. "It seems like all we talk about is high school."

"Do we?" Vi thought about it for a moment. "I guess you're right. Well, we did have a lot of fun."

"We did, but I'd like to get to know you now," Liam said, taking a bite of his rocky road.

Vi wiped her mouth. "What do you want to know?"

"Anything," he replied. "What you loved about New York—"

"Pizza."

"—where you lived—"

"A dump." She grimaced.

He sighed and pushed away his ice cream. "I heard you were going to get married."

Vi paused with a spoonful of ice cream halfway

to her mouth. She let it drop into the bowl and sat back. "Not really."

"Not really?" Liam arched a brow. "That's not much of an answer."

Vi sat up and began to slowly swirl her ice cream with the spoon, not meeting his eyes. "There was someone. I thought we might get married. It didn't work out." She shrugged.

"That's it?"

Vi's jaw tightened. "He dumped me, is that what you want to hear?"

"No, of course not." He reached out and covered her hand with his, but she pulled away, crossing her arms.

Liam ran a hand through his hair in frustration. "Look, I'm sorry," he said. "I didn't mean to bring up a sensitive subject. And I'm sorry that happened to you—"

"It's fine," Vi said tightly, looking out the window. "I'm over it."

"Obviously," Liam said wryly.

Vi stiffened and faced him. "I am," she said firmly. "But just because I'm over it, doesn't mean I want to *talk* about it, okay?"

Liam puffed out a breath. "I get it," he said. "And

I'm sorry. I just—" He looked upward for a moment, considering. "I want us to build something real here, you know? Not something based on high school memories. I want to really know you. Is that so wrong?"

And with that, all of Violet's anger dissipated and she felt like—well, kind of a jerk. "No, it's not," she said in a small voice. I'm sorry." This time, she reached for his hand, squeezing it slightly.

"I'm sorry too," he said.

I'm so, so, so, so

so, so, so, so sorry.

The song popped into her head and she almost laughed out loud. How inappropriate.

"What is it?" Liam asked, his own lips quirking, and she realized she was smiling.

"Sorry." She waved a hand. "It's a song, and—it's nothing."

"What song?" he asked.

"It's dumb," she replied. "Just something Kade and I made up when we were kids."

"Oh." He sat back. "Kade."

"Yeah, it's an *I'm sorry* song." She shook her head. "Like I said, it's dumb."

"Right, well." He cleared his throat. "We're still on for Saturday, right?"

"Of course," she replied. "But Friday first. We're on the decorating committee, remember?"

"How could I forget?"

Vi smiled widely. "Remember that time we were on the committee for the Sadie Hawkins dance?"

And with that, all tension vanished, and the rest of the evening passed in pleasant conversation.

Eleven

Wednesday was a bear of a day. Vi couldn't get her computer to work, so she had to wing a lesson on the history of mime, the kids were wired up about Valentine's Day, and she'd stepped in a puddle on her way into work, so her left foot was cold and clammy all day. On top of that, her male and female leads were absent, so she'd had to run rehearsal with understudies who hadn't bothered to learn the parts yet.

"Everyone knows the understudy never has to do anything," one of them had protested. And Vi couldn't even sum up enough energy to argue the point.

By the end of rehearsal, she was exhausted and irritated. All she wanted to do was go home and crawl in a hot bath, but she and Lena had finally managed to arrange their schedules so they could meet for coffee, and Vi didn't want to cancel on her.

So she walked to the *Daily Grind* and grabbed an

extra-chocolately mocha with extra whipped cream and slumped into a chair across from her friend.

"Whoa," Lena said on a laugh. "What happened to you?"

Lena, of course, looked impeccable, her hair pulled up into a neat ponytail, her clothing clean and dry. Vi made a face at her.

"Teenagers," she muttered. "Teenagers happened to me."

Lena took a sip of her coffee. "Rough day at the office, dear?"

"You have no idea." Vi slid out of her coat and licked the cream off the top of her drink.

"That's a lot of whipped cream," Lena pointed out.

"Don't judge me." She took a sip of the mocha and sighed. "That's just what I needed."

"Coffee and chocolate can cure most of what ails you," Lena said with a smirk, her dimples making an appearance.

"And whipped cream." Vi held up a finger. "Don't forget the whipped cream."

"Of course." Lena tilted her head in a nod. "So, what's new? Well, I mean other than the heathen teenagers tormenting your existence?"

Vi snorted. "Oh, you know. The usual. Mom's all

—" She waved her hands around her head to indicate general craziness. "—about the Sweetheart Ball. Are you going?"

Lena wrinkled her nose. "Nah. I'm going to keep the shop open for all the lonely souls looking to drown their sorrows in hot fudge."

"A true humanitarian."

"I try," Lena said with a smile. "How about you?"

Vi nodded. "Liam asked me," she said, sighing heavily.

"Is that not a good thing?" Lena asked slowly.

"No, it is, I just—" Vi toyed with her coffee cup. "I don't know. I like Liam. I do."

"But . . ." Lena prodded.

"But," Vi said with a slow nod. "There's a but. And I don't know why."

"Well, you haven't been back that long," Lena said. "Maybe you need some time."

"Maybe," Vi said thoughtfully. "I was just so crazy about him back in high school, you know. I guess I expected to feel that way again. That's pretty stupid, now that I say it out loud. Who feels like that when they're our age?"

"Hey, speak for yourself," Lena said in mock outrage. "I'm holding out for the guy who'll sweep me off my feet."

"You think there are a lot of feet-sweepers out there?" Vi asked.

"Definitely." Lena nodded. "Feet sweepers. Stomach tinglers. Hand sweaters."

Vi wrinkled her nose. "Sounds messy."

Lena laughed. "I don't know, Vi. I can't tell you what to do . . ."

"But . . ." Vi said.

"But," she repeated with a smile. "Maybe Liam's not the guy."

Vi considered that, swallowing a mouthful of coffee. "I'm being stupid," she said, setting her cup on the table. "He's perfect for me. He's sweet. Smart. Reliable."

"You make him sound like a golden retriever," Lena said dryly.

Vi threw a wadded up napkin at her. "The point is, I'm being dumb," she said. "I should just go to the ball and stop stressing about all this."

"You really should," Lena agreed. "It's not like you're committing your life to the guy. And if it doesn't work out, there are plenty of other fish in the sea."

Vi snorted. "Oh yeah? Where?" Holiday Junction wasn't exactly a hopping singles scene.

"Maybe right under your nose," Lena said with a mysterious smile, lifting her cup to take another sip.

"Speaking of right under your nose," Vi said, eyeing Lena warily. "I did something that might make you mad."

"What did you do?"

She chewed on her lip. "I tried to get Kade to ask you to the ball so we could double date."

Lena choked on her coffee. "Kade?"

Vi winced. "You're not mad, are you?"

She grabbed a napkin and wiped her mouth. "No, I'm not mad. But why would you try to get *Kade* to ask me?"

"Well, you know, with how you feel about him—"

"How *I* feel about him?" She gaped.

"And how he feels about you—"

"How *he* feels about *me*? Whoa. Back up a second." Lena set aside her coffee cup and leaned her elbows on the table. "You think *I'm* interested in Kade?"

"Well, yeah . . . aren't you?" Vi was getting seriously confused.

"No!" Lena laughed. "Why in the world would you think that?"

"Well—" Vi thought back. "I saw you talking . . .

and laughing. And then he was at the ice cream shop . . ."

Lena looked at Vi like she was crazy. "And that led you to believe I had a crush on Kade? You and I talk and laugh and you come to the shop. That doesn't mean I have a crush on *you*!"

Vi was suddenly questioning everything. "But I thought—" She frowned. "Kade will be devastated."

Lena burst out laughing. "Oh, I seriously doubt that," she said. "Believe me, Kade has absolutely no interest in me."

"But—"

Lena held up a hand. "This time, there is definitely no *but*," she said. "I don't know where you get these crazy ideas, but there is absolutely nothing between Kade and me. Nothing."

"Huh." Vi slumped back in her chair, not understanding how she could have got everything so wrong. "But he said there was someone he was interested in who was interested in someone else. And then when I asked you if that person might be interested, you said yes, so what was that all about?"

Lena only blinked. "Violet, I have absolutely no idea what you're talking about."

"Huh," Vi said again. "Maybe I should talk to Kade about this."

At that, Lena smiled. "That's an excellent idea. You should definitely talk to Kade."

Later that evening, Kade sat on his porch swing, feet propped up on the railing as he strummed his guitar idly. The sky was a clear, indigo blue with a full moon hanging low on the horizon. It was cool, but not freezing, and with the little electric heater running at his feet, he was warm enough. A notepad lay next to him on the swing, scribbled lyrics filling a page, some lines crossed out, others altered so many times he could barely read them anymore.

It didn't matter. Once Kade settled on a lyric, it became part of him. The song burned into his memory like a brand. He remembered every word of every song he'd ever written.

He leaned his head back and closed his eyes, humming along quietly as he played. The song he'd been working on floated through his mind and he sang quietly.

You're right beside me, but so far away

In my arms, but not here to stay

La la la, something something—he was still working on that line.

I've been here all along

"What's that?" a quiet voice asked, and he jerked his head up in surprise. Vi stood leaning on the rail next to his feet. He hadn't heard her approach. She was dressed in jeans and a big lumpy sweater; a blanket over her shoulders.

"Sorry," she said. "Didn't mean to intrude."

"No." He pulled his feet down and sat up. "It's fine. Just working on something new."

She picked up the notebook, but to her credit, didn't look at it before she handed it to him so she could sit next to him, wrapping the blanket tighter around her. "Could I hear some more?"

After all his years songwriting, Kade had overcome any fear of people criticizing his work. And Vi had heard him sing many times. But to have her hear this particular song? Well, it made him more than a little nervous.

"You don't have to," she said quietly.

"No, it's okay," he replied. He strummed a chord and sang what he had so far. A song about loving someone from afar. A song about watching that person walk away.

A song about Vi.

He finished and picked the strings quietly. "That's all I have so far."

Vi smiled. "It's beautiful," she said.

"Well, it's no *I'm so, so, so, so sorry*, but . . ." He shrugged, hoping she wasn't reading too much into it.

She laughed, then leaned her head on the back of the swing, studying him. "It's sad, though."

"They like the sad ones." He strummed the chords again and this time, Vi sang the chorus, her voice carrying out clear and strong.

"Not bad," he said once she finished.

She only smiled in response.

"You ever miss it? Performing?" He picked out some quick scales and Vi smirked.

"Showoff." She leaned back and pushed the swing, her toe brushing the floor. "Sometimes I do miss it," she said. "But, I don't know. I'm not sure New York is right for me."

Kade nearly dropped the guitar. "L.A. then?"

"I don't know anymore." She looked up at him and his breath caught. "To be honest, I'm not sure where I belong."

"You belong here," he said, strumming again in a vain attempt to calm his nerves. "You know that, right?"

She hummed in response. "I could do community theater."

"Or I could write you a song to record, and you could become a big star," he offered.

Vi laughed. "From your lips to God's ears." She tucked the blanket more firmly around her legs. "It's just the longer I'm here, the more I feel connected, you know? Like I'm home."

"It is home."

"Yeah." She yawned and closed her eyes. Kade kept playing and he thought she might have fallen asleep, but after a few minutes she poked him lightly. "Can I ask you something?"

He shrugged a shoulder. "Sure."

"When I first got back, you said you were interested in someone, but that she was interested in someone else."

He could feel her watching him but didn't look at her. "Yeah."

"At first I thought it was Lena."

Kade's fingers fumbled on the strings and he laughed in surprise. "Lena?" He looked at her then, but her eyes were still closed. "So that's why you wanted me to ask her to the ball."

She smiled, and her eyes fluttered open. "I thought it would be fun. Two of my best friends doubling with me and Liam."

Liam. Right.

Kade had almost forgotten about him in his excitement about Vi staying in town. But even if she did, it would be for Liam.

It would be *with* Liam.

"So . . . if it's not Lena, who is it?" she asked.

And this was his chance, wasn't it? His chance to tell her how he felt. His chance to ask her to pick him.

His chance to chicken out like a big, fat, chicken.

He started to play again, bowing his head to look at the strings, and hide his expression. "It's no one you know," he said. "She's from out of town."

"Hmm . . . a city girl? Not really your type."

"Exactly," he murmured, plucking out a new rhythm. "Don't worry about me, though. I'm sure the right one will come along."

"Of course she will," Vi agreed. "And we'll have plenty of double dates."

Kade fought down the heavy feeling in his heart and forced a grin. "Maybe even a double wedding. And our kids will play together and—" He broke off at Vi's stricken expression. "Vi, what is it?"

She sat up and swallowed thickly, wiping at her eyes.

"Oh my—are you crying?" Kade set the guitar aside and reached for her. "Vi, what is it?"

"I'm sorry," she said, inhaling sharply. "I'm fine, really."

"Obviously you're not," Kade pulled away slightly, pushing her hair back from her face. "What's wrong?"

"It's been *months*. I've been fine," she said firmly, and Kade wasn't sure if she was talking to him or herself. "I can't believe I'm falling apart like this."

"Vi, you're scaring me," he said, holding her face so he could meet her gaze. "What happened?"

She moved away and he let her go but held fast to her hand. She swiped the other across her face, taking a few deep breaths. He let her compose herself, and after a few minutes, she squeezed his hand and started to speak.

"I told you about Ben," she said.

"Jerk," Kade spat before he could think better of it. Then he winced. "Sorry."

The corners of Vi's mouth lifted. "No need. He *is* a jerk."

"Is that what you're so upset about?" he asked gently. "Are you missing Ben?"

Vi snorted. "No. That's—no, it's not Ben." She leaned back and started to swing again. "I was pregnant." She let out a heavy breath. "Wow, I've never said that out loud to anyone but my mom."

Kade froze, shocked. "Oh, Vi—"

"I didn't want to tell Ben until I had it confirmed by a doctor," she said, her voice quiet, calm as she looked out over the front yard. "I found out and I was so excited. I thought we were going to get married and be a family and—" She shot a glance at Kade. "Well, that didn't work out so well."

"I didn't even get a chance to tell him," she said. "He told me he was in love with someone else and we were done. I told him later, of course. After I got over the initial shock, I figured he had to know, but —" She shook her head.

Kade's gut churned with rage. He couldn't believe what he was hearing. "I'm so sorry, Vi."

He wasn't sure she heard him. "I was devastated, of course. I cried and raged and man, I hated Ben for a while."

"I don't blame you."

She huffed out a laugh. "But then I decided I was going to come home. I knew Mom would help me with the baby. I'd get back on my feet. Build a life for us." She broke off, her hand flying to her mouth. "But I lost the baby a month later." Tears glistened in her eyes and he couldn't bear it any longer. He slid closer to her and wrapped his arms around her, his cheek pressed against her hair.

"I'm so sorry, Vi."

She shuddered against him and he held her tighter. He wasn't sure how long they sat there, Vi silently weeping as he stroked her hair, but after a while, she pulled away and wiped her cheeks.

"Sorry," she said. "I don't know where that came from."

Kade reached out to touch her cheek. "Don't be sorry. It sounds like something you've been holding onto for a while."

She nodded, wiping her eyes. "Thanks for listening."

Kade pulled her close again. "Are you kidding? Always, Vi. I'll always listen."

"I know." She squeezed him, then let him go, settling back against the swing. "I should go home and go to bed."

"Okay."

"But do you think you can play for me a little longer?" she asked. "Maybe something happy?"

He picked up the guitar and smiled, tapping her on the nose. "You got it."

Kade played and sang, until Violet finally smiled and began to sing along.

After such an emotional evening, Vi should have been exhausted, but she slept well Wednesday night, and woke with the sun Thursday morning. She felt lighter than she had in months, and although she knew losing the baby would stick with her forever, sharing her pain with Kade had helped. He hadn't offered any platitudes or pity. He'd just held her while she cried and it turns out, that was exactly what she needed.

Vi was already in the kitchen with coffee brewing and eggs on the stove when Lou walked in, still in her pajamas.

"Well, you look bright eyed and bushy tailed this morning," Lou observed, pouring herself a cup of coffee.

Vi dished the eggs onto two plates and handed one to her mom. "I do feel pretty bushy tailed, thanks."

"What happened?" They sat down at the breakfast bar, and Vi took a bite before responding.

"I told Kade about the baby last night," she said, the memory still choking her up a bit.

Lou set her fork down. "You did?"

Vi sipped some juice and took a deep breath. "Yeah, I kind of had an emotional moment, and it all came out," she said. "But I think it was good. I feel better."

Lou reached out and squeezed her hand. "I'm glad." Vi knew her mom had been worried about her, even if she didn't press. Lou had known everything, of course, had flown to New York when it happened, despite Vi's insistence she didn't need to. Lou had been there for Vi, as only a mom could be. But since then, Vi hadn't wanted to discuss it, and Lou had respected that.

"Are you okay?" her mom asked, watching her closely.

Vi smiled. "Yeah, I think I am," she replied. "Or I will be, you know?"

Lou patted her hand and went back to her eggs.

Vi spread strawberry jam on her toast. "We went by the Beavers Lodge. I can't believe how beautiful it is now."

"They did a nice job, didn't they?" Lou brushed some crumbs off her fingers.

"They did," Vi agreed. "It's going to be so pretty once it's all decorated for the ball."

"That's the plan," Lou said. "Are you excited about going with Liam?"

"Of course," she said. "It's going to be a lot of fun."

Vi could feel Lou's eyes on her, so she focused on her toast, taking a big bite.

"How are things going with Liam?"

"Great!" She smiled brightly. "Really good. Liam's . . . he's great."

Lou arched a brow. "You said that."

Vi pushed her eggs around on her plate. "Well, he is. And things are going well. He's so sweet to me. I love spending time with him."

"That sounds like a good thing."

Vi nodded. "It is. Liam's perfect for me. He always has been."

"So . . . what's the problem?" Lou asked, pushing her plate away and picking up her coffee cup.

"There's no *problem*, really," Vi replied. "It's just something he said to me has kind of been bothering me a little. Kade mentioned it, too." She turned to face her mom. "Do you think I'm trying to live in the past?"

Lou squinted slightly. "What do you mean?"

Vi inhaled and blew out slowly. "I don't know. Living in my old room. Dating my old boyfriend. Do you think it's weird?"

"Weird? No." Lou shook her head. "But what I think doesn't matter. What do *you* think?"

And that was the rub, wasn't it? Because Violet

didn't know what to think. But maybe talking it out with her mom would help her figure it out.

"I loved Liam in high school," she said, stirring her coffee. "And I know everyone thinks I dumped him, so I'm the bad guy—"

"I don't," Lou said, holding up a finger.

The corner of Vi's mouth lifted. "Thanks, but a lot of people do. And I get that." She set her cup on the counter and turned it slowly. "But it was hard for me, too, you know? I did it because I thought it was the right thing to do. We were so young, and our dreams were leading us in different directions."

"Do you regret it?" Lou asked.

She looked over at her mom. "I don't regret doing it. I do regret hurting him."

Lou pressed her lips together and bowed her head in understanding.

Vi checked the clock. "Shoot. I have to get to work." She got up and carried the plates to the sink.

"And I should shower," Lou said, but she pulled Vi into a hug as she passed her.

"I can't tell you what to do," she said, holding her tight. "But let me give you one word of advice." She pulled back and took Vi's face between her hands.

"Make sure you're with Liam now because you're crazy about him *now*, and not because you're trying to make up for what you put him through *then*." She smiled and kissed Vi's cheek. "Okay?"

Vi nodded. "Okay, Mom."

Lou patted her shoulder and left the room and Vi stared out the kitchen window for a moment, pondering her mother's words, before she headed off to work and tried to put it all out of her mind for a little while.

Twelve

Friday afternoon, the ballroom at the Beavers Lodge was buzzing with activity. Volunteers were unloading boxes of decorations, stringing garland, and setting up tables and chairs when Kade and Vi arrived after school. Vi had been uncharacteristically quiet on the ride over. As a matter of fact, she'd been pretty quiet ever since she told Kade about the baby Wednesday night, but he hadn't pushed. She'd been through a lot and he just wanted to be there for her in whatever way she needed him.

He glanced at her as they walked over to the table where Lou was directing traffic. She looked—well, great, to be honest. Fresh faced and relaxed in a pair of jeans and a fuzzy red sweater.

She caught his look and raised a brow. "What?"

He shrugged. "Nice sweater."

Vi plucked at a sleeve self-consciously. "What's wrong with my sweater?"

"Nothing," he replied, his lips quirking. "I just said it was nice."

Her eyes narrowed. "But you never say anything's nice unless you mean it's decidedly not nice."

And really, he'd been being honest about the sweater, but it was so much fun to mess with her. And comfortable. They fell into it so easily and it seemed to put her at ease.

"You're so paranoid, Chalmers," he said, shaking his head in mock pity. "It's a shame, really."

"It's only paranoia if they're not really out to get you," she pointed out.

He leaned in, waggling his eyebrows. "You think I'm out to get you?"

Vi stilled and she looked at him, her cheeks growing pink and her lips parted slightly. Suddenly, the noise around them softened to a muted hum, and his heart thudded heavily in his chest.

"I—" she said, but it was breathy, like she didn't even mean to say it and it burst out on an exhale. She licked her lips and Kade swallowed, suddenly warm all over.

"Vi—" His gaze locked with hers, her blue eyes shimmering . . . drawing him in . . . pulling him closer.

"Hey guys!" At the familiar voice, Violet startled, the moment broken. Liam appeared next to her and

Kade blinked as he pulled her into his arms and kissed her.

The kiss broke and Liam smiled down at her. "Hi. You look pretty."

Vi smiled up at him, and Kade's stomach dropped to somewhere in the vicinity of his feet. "Thanks." She shot a sideways glare at Kade. "At least some people think so."

He recovered quickly, after years of experience. "I said the sweater was nice!" he exclaimed, throwing up his hands. "I didn't ask what puppet you skinned to get it. Give me some credit!"

Vi made an outraged sound and smacked his arm, as Kade cackled, curling over to protect himself as she tried to hit him again.

Liam watched them with an inscrutable look on his face, then cleared his throat and turned away.

They finally made their way over to Lou, who, despite the frenzy of activity around her, seemed calm as a cucumber.

"Oh good, you're here," she said, flipping through her notebook. "Just in time to put up the lanterns and lights." She picked up a box and handed it to Liam, then placed another in Kade's arms. "Ladders are over there—" She pointed to the far corner. "And you have to use the temporary hooks because we can't put any nails in the drywall."

Kade opened his box to find rolls of white twinkle lights. He immediately checked out Liam's box—the guy was holding up a paper lantern, with a disgusted look on his face. Without a word, he offered his box to Liam and took the other one. Then they retreated to the corner with the ladders.

They worked pretty well together, all things considered. Liam and Kade climbed the ladders and Vi directed things from the floor. It only took an hour or so to get the twinkle lights put up, the strands crisscrossed over the ceiling and dipping down at the corners where they'd eventually be covered by sheer, white fabric. Then they started in on the paper lanterns. This took a little longer because each one had to be opened up, then a tiny LED bulb attached and turned on—since they didn't want to have to go back and turn them all on later.

"A little to the left!" Vi called up to Kade. He was hanging one of the lanterns from a wide beam with fishing line and a little thumbtack—okay'd by Lou since it was in the beam and not the ceiling.

He moved it over. "Here?"

Vi titled her head, considering. "No, a little more."

He complied. "Okay?"

"No, back to the right."

Kade's eyes narrowed, but Vi gazed up at him innocently. He shifted the lantern over.

"No, I was wrong. More to the left." This time, her lips quirked, and the game was up. He stuck the thumbtack into the beam and climbed down the ladder.

"You realize I've been climbing up and down that ladder all afternoon," he said when he approached her. "You could have a little consideration."

"It's good for you," she retorted, handing him a bottle of water. "You could use a little exercise."

He gaped at her. "Are you calling me fat?"

She studied him, up and down, and he had to fight not to fidget. "No, not fat, per se," she said. "Maybe a little . . . puffy?" She poked him in the stomach.

"Puffy?" Kade repeated in outrage. "I'll give you puffy." And with that, he dropped his water bottle and pulled her into a headlock.

"Kade, no!" she squealed, laughing.

"Say it!" He rubbed his knuckles over her head.

Suddenly, Vi shifted on her feet, grabbed his wrist, wrenched it around, and before he knew what was happening, he was flat on his back on the floor, the breath knocked out of him. Vi held his hand by the thumb, his arm slightly twisted. It didn't hurt, but he knew if he moved, it would.

She grinned down at him. "Took a little self-defense while I was away," she said.

"I can see that," he replied.

She tipped her head. "Say it," she said. And the challenge was weighted . . . there was something behind her words that Kade couldn't quite put a name to.

"Guys, is everything okay?" Liam was standing over them, and Vi immediately released Kade, brushing her hands off on her jeans.

"Fine," she said. "Just teaching the King here a few manners."

Kade rolled over on his knees, catching his breath before he stood up. "I hereby concede the crown," he said with a little bow. "Hail to the Queen."

Vi smiled brightly, tipping her head.

"It's looking great, isn't it?" Lou asked, scribbling in her notebook as she approached them. "I think we're just about done, except for the caterers tomorrow. And you'll both be here for the D.J.?" she asked Kade and Vi.

"For the hundredth time, we'll be here, Mom," Vi said, rolling her eyes. "It's all going to be amazing and perfect and wonderful. You made sure of it."

Lou let out a breath, her shoulders relaxing a bit. "Thanks. I just want everything to go well."

"It will."

Lou's gaze shifted to the ballroom entrance. "Oh, what's he doing here?" she muttered, and the group turned to see Joshua Kendricks entering with his entourage—his secretary, Melanie, Boomer Benedict, and Alice Camden, from the Journal bringing up the rear.

The mayor took in the activity, his piercing glance scrutinizing everything from the lanterns overhead to the floral centerpieces. He walked the perimeter of the room, flanked by Melanie and Boomer, instructing the former to take notes, and the latter to quit breathing down his neck.

The group finally came to a stop near Kade and the others, and the mayor took one last sweeping perusal of the room, his mouth pinched.

"I'm not certain it says Valentine's Day," he said.

Everyone gaped—even Boomer Benedict's mouth dropped open in surprise. In addition to the lights and lanterns, three-dimensional paper hearts hung from the ceiling in a variety of sizes. The white tablecloths were topped with squares of sparkling, red fabric, and even the floral centerpieces of red and white roses had little sparkling hearts peeking out from between the blooms.

It didn't only say, Valentine's Day. It shouted it at the top of its lungs.

Lou, to her credit, only asked calmly, though through gritted teeth, "What would you suggest?"

The mayor frowned, the creases around his mouth deepening as he considered the question. "We need more cupids," he said with a firm nod.

"More cupids," Lou repeated flatly.

"Definitely." He turned to Boomer. "Go get the costume."

"Ah, Boss," Boomer said, his shoulders slumped. "You said I wouldn't need it."

"I said you wouldn't need it if the decorations were up to par," Joshua corrected, looking down his pointed nose at him. "They are not, so you will."

Boomer let out a frustrated groan and left the room.

"Costume?" Lou did not look happy. "What costume?"

Joshua smiled. "You'll see." He adjusted his cuffs, and Kade idly noticed how the lantern light reflected off his pomaded, white head.

"Hey," Liam nudged Kade's arm. "You got a second?"

"Uh, sure, I guess," he replied, glancing at Vi. She looked curiously between the two of them, and Liam gave her a peck on the cheek.

"Just need Kade's help with something," he said. "We'll be right back."

"Okay," Vi replied slowly, like she didn't quite believe him, but didn't know how to challenge it. She was quickly diverted by Lou and Joshua's heated conversation debating the value of pink hearts versus red, and Kade walked with Liam out to the lobby.

"What's up?" Kade asked.

Liam took in a deep breath and rubbed the back of his neck as he looked out the window toward the parking lot.

"Look," he said. "This isn't easy to—" He broke off, pressing his lips together, then looked Kade straight in the eye. "I need to ask you a favor."

Kade was surprised but didn't let it show. "What is it?"

Liam hesitated, like he was trying to figure out how to say what he wanted to say. Finally, he squared his shoulders. "We both love Vi, right?" And the way he asked it, it was like he *knew*.

It took all Kade had not to squirm under his scrutiny. "Right," he said.

"And we both want her to be happy?"

"Of course," he said. "Liam, where are you going with this?"

Liam ran his hands through his hair, his gaze going to the ceiling for a moment before he dropped his hands. "I still love Vi," he said. "I don't think I ever stopped. I love her and I want to give her everything. I want to—to marry her one day. Have a family. And I think we could be really good together. I think I could make her happy."

Kade's mouth felt like ash, his heart thudding in his ears. "That's . . ." He swallowed. "That's great."

"But I can't do that, if you're in the way," Liam said.

Kade froze, stunned. "What?"

Liam threw up his hands and paced away a few steps and back again. "I know you're old friends. I get that, and I'm not asking you to give that up—"

"That's good, because there's absolutely no way I would," Kade snapped, anger stiffening his spine, sharpening his tongue. "I'd never abandon her."

"And I'm not asking you to," Liam said, holding up his hands in a placating gesture.

"Then what exactly are you asking?"

Liam faced him, and his face was pleading, his eyes soft. "All I'm asking for is a chance," he said. "A chance to make her see how good we could be again. But when you're always there, teasing her, laughing with her, it makes it tough, you know? Sometimes I feel like an outsider."

And Kade got that. He and Vi did have their own little world sometimes, their own language, almost.

"All I'm asking is for you to step back a little," Liam said, and Kade could tell how much it took for him to ask. "Just give us a chance. Can you do that? For Vi?"

Kade sighed. That was the ticket, wasn't it? He'd do just about anything for Vi. He took a long look at Liam, considering. Vi did really care about him, Kade knew that. And he was a good guy . . . had a good job. A real stand-up member of society.

But most of all, as Kade looked at him, he could see how much Liam cared about Vi.

So, even though it drove an arrow straight through his heart, he forced a smile. "Sure," he said. "Anything for Vi."

Liam nodded, letting out a relieved breath. "Thanks. I—" He shook his head. "Thanks, man." He held out his hand and Kade shook it.

"No problem. I only want her to be happy."

Liam would do that, wouldn't he? He'd make Vi happy. Kade had a flash of Liam and Vi's wedding . . . children running through the lawn next door.

He thought he might be sick.

Instead, he patted Liam on the back. "Now, let's get back to work before Lou sends out a search party."

They walked back into the ballroom and Liam immediately went over to stand next to Vi, sliding an arm over her shoulders as he leaned down to kiss her cheek. She smiled up at him then turned to Kade with a curious look, but he only offered her a small smile in return.

"Oh, you've got to be kidding me!" Lou exclaimed, and everyone turned to see Boomer Benedict walking back into the ballroom dressed in a cupid's costume, complete with a fabric diaper, wings, and a little bow and arrow. Wiry, black hair covered his thick chest and trailed over his shoulders. Even his back had a furry coat, and he wore white socks with black oxford loafers.

It was a vision.

"Boomer, I told you to get waxed!" Joshua exclaimed, as the room broke out into titters. He turned to Lou. "I have three others that will be here tomorrow night, and they will all be smooth as a baby's bottom!" He raised his voice at the end, directing his words toward Boomer.

"Can you believe that?" Vi asked, and Kade was surprised to find her standing right next to him. His eyes immediately sought out Liam, who was still over by the table, watching them closely.

Vi smiled at him, obviously waiting for a smart-aleck comment of some kind, but instead, he just said, "Yeah." He stepped back, waving toward the door. "I've got to run. Forgot I have a lesson. I'll see you later."

Vi looked disappointed, but she nodded. "Okay, see you."

Kade turned and strode out of the ballroom, his stomach in knots.

Something was up with Kade.

Violet waited at the lodge Saturday afternoon, staring out the windows at the swaying grass and mountain range. She and Kade were supposed to meet with David, the D.J. and make sure he had everything he needed for the evening, but Kade was late.

Lou was across the room, talking to the caterers

as they set up serving trays and platters. Vi had planned to drive over with Kade, but he was nowhere to be found, so she'd caught a ride with her mom instead.

It was weird.

She walked along the wall of windows, the mountains in the distance hidden by a bank of clouds. It was supposed to be clear and cold that night, and Vi hoped the weather forecasters were right. Of course, Kade always said—

Kade. Right.

With a thud, her thoughts returned to him. He'd seemed off after his mysterious talk with Liam. Liam had only said he needed Kade's advice for her Valentine's present, so she hadn't pushed him. But she really didn't think that was it. Kade was distant when he returned . . . and he couldn't get out of the ballroom fast enough.

Away from her.

The thought came from nowhere, and it made her stomach flutter a little, a whirl of panicked butterflies.

Then he was gone all day today, his car missing from the driveway, the windows curtained shut. Almost—

Almost like he was avoiding her.

Which didn't make sense at all, of course.

Thinking of Kade made her think of that moment the day before. He'd been teasing her, like he often did, but something was different. He'd said something about getting her, and she'd taken it entirely wrong.

For a moment—just a moment—she thought he might kiss her.

Which didn't make sense either.

Vi crossed her arms, hugging her stomach. Her mind was a whirlwind lately, thoughts of Kade taking weird tangents and strange turns. There were times like yesterday that she thought maybe things were changing between her and Kade, growing into something more.

Then he'd disappear, like today, and she was pretty sure she was imagining things.

Vi sighed and turned away from the window, only to see Kade walking in with the D.J. and carrying a large speaker. He spotted her and nodded.

"We thought you'd set up over here," he told David, directing him to the far wall, next to the dance floor, where they'd set up a large platform. Vi walked over to join them.

"Hello," she said, but David didn't pay her any attention. Instead, he studied the wall, then pulled out a tape measure and ran it along the platform, measuring the length and width—and, inexplicably, the distance from the center to one corner. He got down on his hands and knees to inspect the power outlets, then stood up.

"Very well," he said with a nod. "This will do."

Vi's lips twitched and she shot a glance at Kade, but he didn't seem to notice and only smiled at David. "Great. We'll help you bring everything in."

They loaded in David's equipment, carefully setting it on the platform. David began to walk slowly around the area, humming loudly with his head thrown back.

"Can we help you set up?" Vi asked.

The humming cut off and David looked at her in surprise. "What? Oh . . . no, thank you. I need to study the acoustics in the room to create the proper placement, and it's best if I do it myself." He started to hum again, walking in a circle, and Vi stepped back until she was standing next to Kade.

"Should we go?" she whispered to him.

"I have no idea," Kade replied, watching David in awe. He was making loud clicking sounds, pausing in between as if listening for an echo.

"How important can the acoustics be? He's not the Philharmonic," he said.

"Well, he obviously takes his job very seriously," she replied. "I think it's admirable."

"You would," he said, side-eyeing her.

"And what's that supposed to mean?" She was fighting a smile. This was right. This was the Kade she knew.

He opened his mouth to respond, but then snapped it shut, looking away. "Nothing. Hey, if you've got this, I have some things to do. Can I go?"

Vi blinked at him in surprise. "What?"

Kade backed away from her a step. "I have some other things to do, so if we're done, do you mind if I head out?"

"Uh, no, I guess not," Vi replied, unsure why it left her feeling kind of empty. Sad. "I guess I'll see you tonight?"

"Yeah, sure," Kade said, before turning to leave.

And what. In the world. Was that?

She watched Kade walk away, shoulders stiff and hands jammed in his pockets. He was definitely acting weird, and Vi was done with it. She followed after him and called out his name, but he either didn't hear her, or was ignoring her, because he kept going out the front doors. She quickened her steps until she was running. When she came up behind him and grabbed him by the arm, he spun around, surprised.

"What are you doing?" he asked.

Vi was a little out of breath. "What am I doing? What am *I* doing? What are *you* doing?"

Kade rolled his eyes. "Look, Vi, I really have to go."

"Oh yeah?" she said, eyes narrowed in challenge. "Where?"

"What?"

"Where exactly do you have to go?" she asked. "What has you in such a hurry?"

"I, uh," he looked away. "I have a lesson."

"No, you don't," she said smugly. "You only do lessons on weeknights. Next."

"I don't have time for this." He started toward his car, but she followed him, unable to give up, for some reason.

"What's wrong with you, Kade?" she asked. "What happened yesterday with Liam?"

That stopped him in his tracks. "What?" He glanced back at her. "Nothing happened with Liam."

"Then why are you being so weird?" she asked. A rumble of thunder sounded in the distance and she glanced up at the darkening clouds. "It's like you're avoiding me."

He turned to face her. "I'm not avoiding you," he said. "I just have other things to do, you know. It's not all about you, Vi."

She felt as if he'd slapped her. "I never said it was."

"I can't be there at your beck and call, you know," he spat. "Besides, isn't that Liam's job?"

Vi's cheeks flushed with anger. "So, this *is* about Liam."

"It's not about Liam," he said, fisting his hair. "It's about you and me." He jabbed a fingertip into his own chest. "I can't do this anymore."

Soft raindrops began to fall, pelting her face, but Vi barely felt them. "Can't do what?" she asked quietly.

"I can't—" He looked up, the rain flattening his hair. "I can't be there for you. Not like I have been. I can't sit on the swing with you when you cry and make jokes with you and sing songs with you. I just can't do it anymore."

"Why not?" she asked, her heart pounding, the raindrops mixing with tears.

"I just can't," he said, his jaw tightening. Water dripped down his nose, and he swiped it away. "I can't be your friend, Vi. Not like I used to be. Not anymore."

She grabbed his arm again, her fingers digging into the wet cotton of his jacket. "You can't say that and walk away. Not without a reason. Not without an explanation!"

"There's no place for me, Vi," he said firmly. "You and Liam—"

"What are you talking about?" She shook her head. "Just because I'm with Liam doesn't mean we can't—"

"But it *does*!" His voice was pleading. "You can't have us both. It's not like high school."

"But why?"

"Because it's not!" he shouted.

But Violet was angry, too. Angry and confused. "Tell me why!" she shouted. "Give me a good reason."

"Vi—" He tried to pull away, but she held fast.

"Tell me why!"

He looked at her, eyes wild and frenzied, and he took hold of the hand gripping his arm. "Because I'm in love with you!"

Vi stared at him, stunned.

"I've always been in love with you," he said, his own eyes filling with tears. "Even back then. And back then, I could do it. I could stuff it down and be your friend. Watch you with Liam and be there for you however you needed me. But now? Now it's so much . . . *more.* And I can't do it, Vi. I can't watch you with Liam and wait on the porch until you need someone to talk to. I can't. Do. It." He squeezed her hand gently and pulled it away from his arm and she let him.

He turned to head to his car, but looked back at her, over his shoulder. "I'm sorry," he muttered.

And Vi stood in the parking lot of the Beavers Lodge in the middle of a rainstorm and watched Kade drive away, adrift on a wave of shock and despair.

Thirteen

What had he done?

Kade stood behind the refreshment table at the Sweetheart Ball, putting on a smile and pouring out cups of punch. Everyone was having a wonderful time, but Kade felt like his tie was choking the life out of him.

Or perhaps that was regret.

He told her.

He told her.

He hadn't intended to do it. After his little talk with Liam, he planned to lay low, try to let things work out on their own. Eventually, he and Vi could go back to some semblance of a friendship, even if they weren't as close as they once had been. The thought made him feel lost, empty, but Liam was right. Kade could give Vi what she wanted . . . because *Liam* was what Vi wanted.

But when he saw her, eyes sparkling with laughter as she watched the D.J. do his ridiculous tests, his heart had broken inside his chest, and he knew he couldn't be near her, knowing she could never be his.

Not anymore.

So he'd tried to leave. Like the good guy. Like the gentleman. But she'd been stubborn and pushy and in the end, well . . .

He'd told her. And now he very well could face the rest of his life without Vi in it. Like a coward, he'd even hidden out the rest of the afternoon in his classroom at school, afraid to run into her at home.

What was he thinking? Maybe he could take it back. He could tell her—what, exactly? How did one take back, *I'm in love with you.*

Nope. Kade had to face facts: He'd ruined everything.

"Can I have a little more?" Lou stood across the table from him, holding out her cup.

"Of course." He filled it and she took a sip. She wore a gray gown with slitted sleeves and little gemstones at the shoulder.

"You look nice tonight, Lou."

She smiled at him. "Thanks. You clean up pretty good yourself."

He looked down at his own dark suit. The only one he owned, in fact. "Thanks. Good turnout," he said. "Looks like everyone's enjoying themselves."

Lou hummed, nodding. "I could do without the cupids, though."

Boomer Benedict and three other guys—football players from the high school—wore diapers and wings, weaving between the tables and miming shooting people with their arrows.

"I don't know," Kade said. "At least Boomer waxed his back."

Lou grimaced. "I suppose we should be grateful for small favors." She glanced at him. "Have you seen Vi? I thought she and Liam would be here by now."

Kade stirred the punch, watching the ripples. "Nope."

"Oh, there they are," Lou said, looking toward the entrance.

Kade followed her gaze and his breath caught.

Vi's shoulders were bare, except for the tiny straps of a pink dress with a full skirt . . . white at the top, fading into almost magenta at the hem, with white flowers weaving from one shoulder across the bodice and down the skirt. Her blonde hair was caught up into a complicated knot, a few strands framing her glowing face. She was smiling up at Liam, and he leaned down to kiss her forehead.

She was absolutely stunning. And Kade couldn't breathe.

Vi looked in his direction and he realized Lou was waving her over. The fluttering twist of his stomach made him feel slightly nauseated, and he hoped he wouldn't throw up in the punch bowl.

With a faint smile, Vi started toward them, and Kade panicked. What would he say to her? How could this not be horribly, awfully weird?

But then Liam caught her arm and whispered something in her ear. She glanced over at Kade, brow furrowed, but followed Liam to the other side of the room to talk to another couple.

Kade didn't know if he should feel relieved or disappointed.

"You okay, sweetie?" Lou was watching him with concern.

"I, uh." Kade wiped sweat off his upper lip. "You know what, Lou? I'm not feeling so well. Would you be okay without me?"

She tipped her head, sympathy evident on her features. "Of course. I'll get someone else over here. Maybe Boomer. Keep him from scaring the guests with that arrow." She reached out and touched his cheek. "You sure you're okay?"

"Yeah." Kade nodded but didn't meet her eyes. "I just need to get some sleep, I think."

"Okay," she said quietly.

He hooked the ladle handle on the edge of the punch bowl. "Have a good evening."

"You too," Lou said, "And Kade?" When he finally looked at her, she smiled. "Don't give up."

He didn't even ask her what she meant by that. He just got out of the ballroom as quickly as he could, making sure to stay far away from Vi as he went.

Violet pasted on a smile and nodded at the woman speaking to her. Her date was a colleague of Liam's, so they were chatting about a case or something—Vi wasn't really paying attention—and she was left to discuss fashion choices with—

What was her name again? Tasha? Wanda?

Vi couldn't even remember. She was so surprised to see Kade behind the punch bowl when she walked in that she couldn't keep another thought in her head. She'd wanted to go over and talk to him but, to be honest, she had no idea what to say. His confession had knocked her off her feet, and she was still stunned when she thought about it.

"And so I couldn't decide between pink and red," Wanda/Tasha said. "But when I saw this little number, I couldn't say no."

Vi eyed her outfit and had to admit that *little number* fit it perfectly. The skin-tight, red-sequined dress was cut low at the top and high at the bottom, her long legs on prominent display as she balanced on matching high heels. And every inch of her not covered with sequined spandex was coated with sparkly glitter.

"Well, you look amazing," Vi said. "I definitely couldn't pull that off."

"Oh, you're sweet," she said. "The secret is Pilates. And no carbs . . ." And with that, she launched into a discourse on diet and exercise, and Vi's thoughts wandered again.

Kade was in love with her. Her best friend. Her partner in crime since she was a little girl. And she'd had absolutely no idea.

She felt like an idiot. A self-absorbed, narcissistic idiot.

Vi tried to sneak a peek over at the refreshment table, but she couldn't see Kade, at least not without turning her head, giving away the fact that she wasn't paying attention.

"Oh!" Wanda/Tasha let out a little squeal, and Vi noticed she was holding an arrow with a heart-shaped tip. "He shot that right at me," she told Vi. "He could have poked my eye out!"

Vi sincerely doubted that, but she put on what she hoped was a sympathetic expression. "Are you all right?"

"Well, yes. Thank goodness." The woman's hand fluttered over her cleavage, the extremely low neckline leaving little to the imagination. Vi wondered how she was keeping everything in.

Boomer Benedict wandered over and held out his hand. "Sorry," he said. "That one got away from me a bit."

Vi bit her lip to keep from laughing. Per the mayor's instructions, Boomer had waxed his back—it was smooth and hairless, and Vi kind of felt sorry for Boomer. It must have been painful. His chest, however, was still covered with wiry black hair from his shoulders down to his white cotton diaper. The straps from his wings were a little too tight, cutting into his shoulders, and he'd added a gold circlet to his comb over, which slipped a little, so he kept shoving it back up.

"You should be more careful," Wanda/Tasha said, handing him the arrow.

Boomer grunted, mesmerized by her cleavage—maybe it was the glitter—and she snapped her fingers in front of his face to get his attention.

"Sorry, Rose." *Huh. Not even close with her name.*

While Rose was distracted, Vi tried to scope out the refreshment table again. People kept passing in front of her, however, so she couldn't get a clear sight-line. Frustrated, she finally turned back to Rose, who was scolding a withering Boomer.

"I'll be right back," she said. "I'm just going to go get something to drink." She wasn't sure what she'd say to Kade, but she had to see him. Tell him she was sorry for being so insensitive. Promise to be better if he'd just give her another shot.

She squared her shoulders and was about to cross the room when Liam appeared next to her, his hand at the small of her back.

Liam. She'd almost forgotten all about him.

"Hungry?" he asked, his blue eyes warm as he smiled down at her.

"Um, yeah," she said. "I could eat."

They started toward the table and he leaned down to say quietly. "Thanks for that. I wasn't sure how to get away from Lucas. I forgot how worked up he gets talking about work. I've never met anyone so passionate about bankruptcy law."

She snorted. "Sounds exciting."

"You have no idea." He pressed his lips to her temple. "Did I tell you how beautiful you look tonight?"

She smiled. "You might have mentioned it." Vi reached up to smooth the lapel of his dark blue suit. Liam was clean shaven, his sandy hair styled impeccably. "You look pretty nice yourself."

They neared the refreshment table and Vi scanned the area, searching for Kade, but he was nowhere to be found.

"Something wrong?" Liam asked.

"Huh?" Vi blinked, then shook her head. "Oh, no. I was just looking for Kade. I thought I saw him over here earlier."

Liam's jaw tightened. "Oh, well I'm sure he's around here somewhere." He reached for a couple of plates and handed her one. "The beef looks good."

Vi took the plate. "Thanks." They walked slowly down the table, filling their plates. "We just had kind of a—" *what would she call it,* "—fight, this afternoon? I wanted to make sure he's okay."

Liam took a roll and set the tongs down on the

platter, a little hard. "Well, you can always call him tomorrow. Or you'll see him at school Monday, right?"

"Yeah, I guess." Vi scooped up some fruit salad, even though she didn't really want any.

"Look," Liam turned to face her. "I know you're worried about him, but Kade's a grown man. I'm sure he's fine. You guys will work it out. You always do. Maybe he just needs a little space."

Vi wasn't sure she agreed, but she nodded anyway.

"Now, can we find a table and try to enjoy our evening?" he asked, flashing her that dazzling smile that, in the past, had made her weak in the knees.

Funny. Her knees felt just fine. Solid as a rock.

"Of course," she said with a half-shrug. "You're right. I'm sure he's fine."

They found a table near the dance floor and Vi tried to focus on Liam and having a good time. She smiled and laughed in all the right places, but in the back of her mind, she was still worried about Kade. She couldn't help it.

"Where did your mom find this D.J.?" Liam asked, once they'd finished eating and were sipping champagne, watching the dancers. Despite David's eccentricities, he was doing a great job. He wore a simple black tux and was sticking to the classic playlist.

"Well, it's no Disco Retro Glam Funk, but it's all right," she quipped.

"Huh?" Liam looked confused.

"Oh, nothing," she said, sweeping back a loose strand of hair. "Just something he said when we met with him. It's—nothing. It was funny at the time." Her voice drifted off and she really hoped Liam would drop it.

He did. The song changed to a slow, Sinatra track, and he stood, holding out his hand. "Care to dance?" he asked.

"Sure," she said, taking his hand. He led her out to the middle of the dance floor and slipped an arm around her waist, the other holding her hand loosely. They swayed to the music, and Vi rested her head on his shoulder.

"This is nice," she murmured.

He hummed in agreement, giving her a little squeeze.

And it was. Being with Liam had always been nice. Comfortable.

Safe.

And after everything she went through with Ben, safe was what she wanted . . . what she needed.

"Hey, I was thinking," Liam began, and Vi straightened to face him. "My parents are coming to visit in a couple of weeks. I thought we could have dinner together. I know they'd love to see you again."

She smiled. "That would be nice."

"They were happy to hear you were back," he said, turning her in a small circle. "Well, thrilled would be more like it. You wouldn't believe it. Mom actually mentioned grandchildren."

A sudden chill ran down Vi's spine. "Grandchildren?" she squeaked.

"Of course, I was quick to point out that you just got here. That's somewhere way off in the future, but she was just excited, I think." He twirled her under his arm, and back again.

And in a dizzying blur, it all flashed before her eyes—a life with Liam . . . marriage, children. A little house on the edge of town. Camping trips and parent-teacher conferences.

"So don't get scared off if she mentions marriage," he said, rolling his eyes. "I warned her not to push you, but you know my mom—"

Birthdays. Anniversaries. Family movie nights and candlelight dinners. Like a slideshow, she saw it all, and with a sickening thud in the pit of her stomach she realized she wanted all of it.

She just didn't want it . . . with *Liam*.

Vi stopped in the middle of the dance floor and stepped back, her hands flying to her mouth, her breathing uneven.

"Vi? Are you okay?"

What was she doing? "I'm sorry," she gasped out, a wave of dizziness sweeping through her. "I can't—"

"Come on," Liam said, wrapping an arm around her waist and leading her off the dance floor to a chair in the corner. She sat down, and he pulled over another chair so he could face her. "Breathe, Vi. Try to breathe slowly."

She did, in and out, and after a few moments, she looked at Liam with tears in her eyes.

"Liam, I'm so sorry. I can't do this."

"It's okay, I'll take you home," he said, moving to get up.

"No." She lay a hand on his knee, stilling him. "I mean, *us*. I can't—" She swallowed. "I can't do us."

He looked stunned, but just for a moment, the expression quickly morphing to resignation. "I know," he sighed.

"You do?"

Liam's head hung forward. "I've known for a while, but I just hoped—" He leaned back, and ran his fingers through his hair, then let his hands drop into his lap.

"I'm so sorry," she said. "I haven't been fair to you. Then or now. I left you—"

"That doesn't matter," he said. "I got over it."

"But it does," she said firmly, the tears flowing freely now. "I hurt you and I'm so sorry, Liam."

He looked at her for a long moment, then nodded, his own eyes glistening. "I thought I could be the one, you know? I thought, given enough time —" His shoulders slumped and he leaned forward, his elbows on his knees as he met her gaze. "But it's Kade, isn't it? He's the one."

Vi opened her mouth to say no, of course not. But then she saw another slideshow . . . all the same pictures, but with Kade, instead of Liam. Kade waiting for her at the end of the aisle. Kade holding her baby. Kade laughing with her while they watched a horrible movie on TV.

And she couldn't deny it.

She wanted it all . . . with Kade. She wanted to sit on the porch swing with him. Do goofy dances and sing stupid songs with him. Eat Jell-O tuna pie and hang paper lanterns and prune bushes . . . laugh and cry and live and love . . .

With Kade.

And it hit her like a strike of lightning—she was in love.

With Kade.

"Oh," she whispered, fingers pressed to her lips.

Liam huffed. "You didn't even realize it, did you?"

She shook her head violently, tears still flowing down her cheeks.

"For a smart girl, you can be pretty dumb." The corner of his mouth turned up.

Vi gave a strangled laugh. "Super dumb."

He reached over and took her hands in his. "So now that you know, what are you going to do about it?"

"I—" What was she going to do? She was in love with Kade—the thought settled along her bones, warming her.

She was in love with Kade.

And Kade—

She inhaled sharply. Kade was in love with her.

Oh.

Kade told her he was in love with her, and she'd said nothing. *Nothing.* She'd let him leave without saying a word and who knew what he was thinking now?

She jumped to her feet. "I have to go find him," she said.

"There you are," Liam said, releasing her hands. "I was wondering when you'd figure it out."

Vi turned and ran away a few steps, then whirled around and returned to Liam. "I'm so sorry."

"Stop saying that," he said, rolling his eyes. "I'm fine. Just go." He made a shooing motion with his hands.

Vi hesitated for only a moment before throwing her arms around Liam's neck. "Thank you," she whispered.

He embraced her gently. "You're welcome."

She pulled away and gave him a soft smile before she turned to head quickly across the dance floor. She spotted her mother and dodged through the dancing couples to get to her.

"Mom, can you get a ride home? I need to borrow your car."

Lou gave her a knowing look and reached under the table for her purse, withdrawing her keys. "Don't speed," she warned.

"Wouldn't dream of it," Vi said, crossing her fingers behind her back. She grabbed the keys and raced toward the parking lot.

Lou grabbed two glasses of champagne off the table before she made her way to the corner where Liam Durant was sitting, staring aimlessly into space.

"You look like you could use a drink," she said, offering him one of the glasses.

He took it, raising it in a silent salute before taking a long gulp.

She sat down next to him, watching the dancers for a moment. "That was a good thing you did."

He snorted. "Then why do I feel like crap?"

Lou patted him on the knee. "It'll pass."

He made a noncommittal noise, and Lou smiled. "It will. Your time will come, Liam Durant."

"How can you be so sure?"

She looked at him, straight in the eye. "Because you're a good man," she said. "And good men don't end up alone."

Lou leaned back a little, crossing her ankles and they sat in silence for a moment.

"Thanks, Lou," he murmured.

"Don't mention it." She held up her glass and he clinked his against it. Then they relaxed for a while, sipping champagne, and enjoying the music.

Fourteen

Kade sat on the front porch swing with the guitar across his lap, but he hadn't played a note. No, he was wallowing, as evidenced by the half-empty pizza box, crumpled bag of cheese curls, and carton of melting ice cream sitting on the floor.

Yes, Kade wallowed like a teenage girl. No, he didn't care.

He sat in the darkness—he hadn't even bothered to turn on the porch light—and leaned his head back, watching the stars he could see peeking out beyond the edge of the roof. He pushed the swing idly, the chains creaking as it moved. He thought about giving up for the day and going to bed, but every time he closed his eyes, he saw Vi, a vision in pink, practically glittering under the twinkle lights at the Sweetheart Ball, and nerves and regret would rear their ugly heads once again.

He'd ruined everything. But at the same time, he wasn't sure he could have done anything differently.

It was a difficult position to be in, especially considering he had to face her every day.

For the rest of his life.

Sure, maybe he was being a little dramatic. Kade knew they would get past this, eventually. People did all the time, right? They'd move on. Maybe even be friends again.

But he knew it would never be the same. So, in addition to the humiliation of proclaiming his love for someone who didn't love him back, he'd also lost a friend. The thought left him feeling hollow and depressed.

Hence, the wallowing.

Kade sighed and took a long swallow of orange soda, the sweetness making him wince. He dropped the empty bottle onto the porch floor, where it rolled off the edge and thumped into the damp grass. He'd get it later. A flash of headlights made him sit up, and he saw Lou's car pull into the driveway next door. It was odd, her leaving the ball so early, and he hoped something wasn't wrong. He was about to get up and walk over to check on her but froze when he saw who got out of the car.

Vi. And she was looking right at him.

Kade's heartbeat quickened, and he thought for a

moment about running, just getting up, going inside, and locking the door—pretending he hadn't seen her. But he hesitated a moment too long, and Vi crossed the small strip of lawn separating the two yards, her heels clicking lightly as she walked over his driveway. She came up the walkway, but paused at the bottom of the stairs, looking up at him from the shadows.

"Hi," she said.

Kade swallowed thickly. "Hi." He couldn't see her eyes in the darkness, only a vague outline of her illuminated by the street light. "How was the ball?"

She tipped her head. "You left early."

He glanced at his watch. "So did you."

She seemed to take a deep breath, then climbed the steps. Now that she was closer, he could make out her features a little better, see her faint smile and the way she twisted her fingers together in front of her. Was she nervous?

Her gaze dipped briefly to the floor around him. "Looks like quite the party."

"Yeah, well." Kade's head spun, and for the life of him, he couldn't think of a witty comeback. "What are you doing here, Vi?"

She bit her lip. "I needed to talk to you." She came closer, but didn't sit next to him, just leaned back against the porch rail, facing him. After a moment, she winced and kicked off her shoes, flexing her bare toes against the wood floor. Her toenails were pink.

"That's better," she said. "Whoever invented high heels should be drawn and quartered."

"Pretty sure he or she is already dead," Kade pointed out.

Vi shrugged. "Technicalities." They smiled at each other and Vi pressed her lips together and looked away.

"Where's Liam?" Kade asked, and then wished he hadn't. He didn't want to talk about Liam. He wanted Vi to sit on the swing with him . . . to wrap them both in a blanket and forget about everything—and everyone—else.

"Liam . . ." Vi looked up, blinking rapidly for a moment. "Liam is—" She looked suddenly sad, and Kade set his guitar aside, standing up.

"Is he okay? Did something happen?"

"Oh no, he's fine, I—" She covered her face with her hands for a moment, then swept them back over her hair. "I'm not doing this very well."

"It's okay, I know I made things awkward between us," Kade said, moving to stand next to her, his hip against the rail as he studied her profile. "I'm sorry about that, Vi. I don't know what I was thinking—"

"No, Kade—"

"I was just freaking out, I mean with you and Liam getting back together—maybe I was feeling a little left out—"

"Kade—"

"But I didn't mean it, okay?" He took both of her hands in his, holding them gently. "You're the most important person in my life, Vi. And I love you, I do, but I can get past that, if you let me. I'll be *fine*." He shook her hands once to emphasize the word. "I didn't mean it when I said I couldn't be your friend anymore. Of course I want to be your friend, if you'll let me."

He looked into her blue eyes, sparkling with unshed tears, and prayed she'd forgive him. Because there was no way he could go on without her in his life. Vi blinked and the tears trickled down her cheeks, and she dipped her head, looking at their joined hands.

"No," she whispered, and a heavy feeling settled in Kade's stomach.

"What?" He tried to release her hands, but she held fast. "No?"

"No, I can't do that," she said, then she met his

gaze, a hopeful smile on her face. "Because I want more."

Kade blinked, unable to process what she was saying for a long moment. His heart began to thump hard within his chest, hope unfurling like the first spring flower. "What?" he whispered.

"You've been my best friend my whole life," she said, her smile growing, even through the tears. "You made me laugh. You held me when I cried. You were always there for me—you still are—and I was so stupid and blind I didn't even realize—" She shook her head with a small laugh. "I think about you all the time. When something funny happens at school, it's you I want to share it with. And when the bad things happen—" Her face darkened for a moment, and he knew she was thinking about the baby. "—you're the one who makes it better. And I've been so selfish, and I'm sorry, so sorry for that—"

"Vi, what are you saying?" He thought he understood, but after all this time, he didn't dare read too much into things. He didn't think he could take it if he was wrong. Still, he couldn't keep down the hope growing in him, a warmth weaving its way through his heart.

"Oh, I can't believe I'm messing this up so badly,"

she moaned, releasing him to cover her face again. Then, she took a deep breath, and lowered her hands, meeting his gaze with an almost stubborn look on her face.

"I love you," she said firmly. "And I know I've said it in the past as a friend, but I want to make this perfectly clear. I'm *in love* with you." She waved her hands in a broad gesture. "Like a man loves a woman. All the marbles. In like Flynn. For better or for worse." She blushed. "I mean, not *that* obviously, because *for better or for worse* would be down the road, but yeah. Like that, too. Eventually." She nodded once.

When he stared at her for a moment, she shifted nervously, her eyes cutting to the side. "And if you could say something, that would be *awesome.*"

He stepped toward her, his heart racing, nerves tingling, every inch of his body awake and so, so alive. "I already told you I loved you."

Her lips twisted to the side. "So you only have to say it once? Because I have to say, if this relationship is going to work—"

"Relationship?" He smirked, reaching out to touch her face. "Is that what we have?"

She rolled her eyes but pressed her cheek into his

palm. "You're really going to make me work for this, aren't you?"

"Maybe." He pulled her close, his hands on her waist. "So you *like* me, like me?"

"I'm not so sure anymore," she said haughtily, but her lips twitched.

"If I send you a note, will you check yes or no?"

"I'll wad it up and throw it right at your head, you obnoxious jerk." But she wrapped her arms around his neck, so he knew she was kidding.

Kade laughed, the joy bursting out of him. He leaned in, his lips only separated from hers by a breath. "I love you," he said softly. "I'll love you forever."

He kissed her, then, and his whole body lit up, electricity racing along his nerve endings, his heart pounding so loudly, he wondered if she could hear it. He could feel her, soft and warm, pressed against him, the scent of vanilla and flowers making him dizzy. He shifted, his hands going to her face, tangling in her soft hair as he deepened the kiss. She sighed, and he could feel it in his soul, the echo of it vibrating through him. When he finally pulled back to catch his breath, her eyes were closed, her lips moist and parted, cheeks flushed, and he felt like—he *knew* he wanted to look at that face forever. On the porch swing, at the dinner table—every night and every morning.

Finally, her eyes fluttered open, warm and knowing, and she smiled at him with joy and love.

He had to admit, his knees felt a little weak.

"Want to sit for a bit?" he asked roughly.

"Yeah," she said. "You got any of that pizza left? I'm starving!"

Kade laughed and they settled on the swing, sharing the last of the cold pizza and orange soda, talking about nothing in particular, and looking up at the stars. It was like so many evenings they'd spent together in the past, with a few more kisses added in for good measure, of course.

Kade had almost feared that they'd lose this, their easy friendship, along the way. But in that moment, he realized that their love was *built* on friendship. It was integral, the two interconnected and woven together over the years. And it would only get stronger as they walked this new path together.

Vi snuggled up to him and he wrapped his arm over her, pulling her close as they rocked in the swing. Kade pressed a kiss to the top of her head. "So what now?" he asked.

"Oh, Kade, I'm surprised you haven't figured it out already," she said, looking up at him with a sunny smile. “This is the part where we live happily ever after.”

He snorted. “You’re so corny.” And she giggled.

But as he pulled her into another kiss, he began to believe that that's exactly what they would do.

Epilogue

Three Months Later

Violet walked into McKenna's Creamery and scanned the room looking for Kade. She didn't see him, so she went up to the counter and ordered their usual from Lena.

"How's everything going?" Lena asked as she dished up their ice cream.

"Really great," Vi replied. "School's going well, and I think the spring musical is going to be excellent."

"That's fantastic," Lena said, sliding a dish across the counter toward her. "How's Kade?"

"Kade is good," Vi said, smiling faintly. "He's supposed to meet me here to celebrate something, although he won't say what it is."

"Ugh, look at you with your dreamy, heart eyes." Lena wrinkled her nose. "It's gross."

Vi grabbed a few napkins out of the dispenser.

"Hey, you're one to talk!" she said. "I've been seeing some hearts in those eyes lately, too."

Lena blushed. "Yeah, but we're not talking about *me* right now."

Not to be deterred, Vi asked, "What's it been, about two months? I bet your mom's ready for a wedding."

"Ugh, she won't let up," Lena confided. "It's like she thinks I'm an old maid who better lock it up or I'll be left old and alone with a houseful of cats." Her gaze flickered behind Vi for a second. "But enough about me. There's your prince charming now."

Vi turned and spotted Kade walking into the shop, dark hair glinting in the spring sun coming in through the windows. He lifted a hand in a wave, then pointed to a table near him. She told Lena they'd talk later, carried over the ice cream, and set the bowls on the table, taking a seat next to him.

He leaned over and kissed her. "Hi."

She blushed, still unable to prevent it when he looked at her like that. "Hi." Vi smiled at him for a moment, lost in his dark eyes, just a little bit.

"Okay, so what's this surprise you're being so mysterious about," she said finally, scooping up some ice cream. "I'm dying with curiosity."

He folded his hands on the table. "Well, you know that song we recorded?" It was the one he'd been writing that Vi had thought was so sad. Kade finally finished it and roped Vi into singing the demo. He'd told her the reception was positive, so she supposed he was right—they liked the sad ones.

"Does someone want to buy it?" She held up two fists, ready to cheer if what she guessed was correct.

"Not exactly," Kade said slowly. "I heard back from a producer I know, and he says he's definitely interested. In you."

He held his hands up in a victory V, a wide smile on his face.

"Really?" It had been a long shot, they both knew it, but Kade had sent the demo out to a few of his contacts, to see if there was any interest in signing Vi to a record deal. She pressed her fingers to her lips. "He wants to work with me?"

"Both of us, really," Kade replied. "He wants to record the single and shop it around a bit. If it does well, they might want a full album."

"An album?" Vi couldn't believe it.

He grabbed her hand. "This could be it, Vi. Your chance to finally be a star."

She looked into his eyes, a feeling of peace

settling in her heart. "I don't care about that anymore, to be honest" she said. "But if we can do this together, that'd be so much fun!"

He grinned. "Yeah, it would be."

They talked about all the possibilities, albums and tours and music festivals. It would be crazy, but Vi knew they could handle it. Kade had managed to have it all—a home in Holiday Junction, his teaching career, and music. She was sure she could, too, as long as he was by her side.

They finished their ice cream and waved goodbye to Lena before walking outside. HJ was decorated for spring with pots of bright flowers everywhere and garlands of bright green leaves. They held hands as they walked toward the town square, enjoying the warmth of the bright, sunny day.

"So, I have something for you," Kade said, lifting their joined hands to press a kiss to her fingertips.

"Oh yeah? You got me a present?"

"Yeah, uh . . ." He reached into his jacket pocket, not meeting her eyes. "I know this is early, but it's not what you think, so don't freak out or anything."

Vi was offended. "I never freak out!"

Kade rolled his eyes. "Right." He laughed and pulled out a small box, offering it to her.

Her heart thudded. Was this—Could it be—

She licked her lips and pulled loose the white ribbon, tucking it into her own pocket. She glanced up at him before opening the box, only to reveal a jeweler's box inside.

"Kade," she whispered.

"Like I said, don't freak out." He took the outer box and shook the jeweler's box free, handing it to her.

She opened it slowly, gasping at the ring nestled on the velvet inside. It wasn't huge, but it was beautiful, a round ruby in the center, flanked by three tiny diamonds on each side. It looked familiar.

"Is this—"

Kade nodded. "It was my mother's," he said. "And like I said, it's not what you think. I mean, it's way too early for us to get engaged, right? But I thought. I mean, you and I, I think we're forever. And eventually we will get engaged. So this is for that. To be engaged to be engaged, or whatever." He reddened, rubbing the back of his neck, and Vi found his nerves adorable.

Vi smiled. "We are," she said. "Forever, I mean."

"Right?" His shoulders relaxed a bit. "So I wanted to give you something that showed you I was thinking about it, but I know it's too soon, so—"

"It's not," she said.

He blinked at her. "Not what?"

She tipped her head and picked a piece of invisible lint off his sleeve. "Too soon."

Vi looked up at him, waiting patiently as the gears worked.

"So you think . . ." He swallowed.

"I do." She giggled. "Get it?" She nudged him with her elbow.

He didn't laugh but studied her carefully. "You're sure?"

She popped up on her tip toes and kissed him softly, the box pressed between them. "I'm sure. So sure." She hesitated, looking warily into his eyes. "If you are."

"I am!" he exclaimed. "I so am." He grabbed the box from her and plucked the ring out, pinching it between two fingers. "I have to do this right." He dropped down onto one knee, and Vi's heart soared, tears of joy pricking at her eyes.

Kade cleared his throat and looked up at her, holding the ring before him. "Vi, I've loved you for as long as I can remember," he said, "and I can't imagine my life without you."

Vi clasped her hands together, trying to resist grabbing him and kissing him before he was finished.

His own eyes glimmered with unshed tears, but his voice was strong. "I want to build a life with you, raise a family with you, make music together, and even your ridiculous swing dances—"

"They're not ridiculous," she protested.

"If you don't mind," Kade said, holding up a finger. "Proposing here."

Vi pressed her lips together. "Sorry. Please continue." She waved a magnanimous hand.

Kade winked at her. "I already told you I'd love you forever, so I guess this just makes it official. You and me. All the marbles. In like Flynn. For better or for worse."

Vi let out a joyous laugh, hearing her own words said back to her.

"So . . . I'm asking you, Violet Chalmers," he said, offering the ring with a dazzling smile that definitely made her weak in the knees. "Will you marry me?"

And, of course, she could only say one thing. "Yes!"

He gave a loud whoop and jumped to his feet, then slid the ring onto her finger. She admired it for a moment, the way the stones glinted in the sunlight, then she threw herself into his arms. "I can't believe we're engaged!" she said, throwing her head back and laughing as he swung her around in a circle.

"Believe it," he said, setting her back on her feet. "You're committed now. There's no going back."

He kissed her, and in it she could feel everything between them—the friendship and love, the joy and hope for the future.

She looked up at him, her heart full, and said, "We should go tell my mom."

He agreed, and they turned to head toward the bookstore.

"Can you believe she's taking credit for us getting together?" Vi asked. "She says it was part of her plan all along."

Kade laughed. "Well, I guess it doesn't hurt to let her believe that.

And as the two of them made their way down Main Street, sharing kisses and plans for the life they'd create together, the three women dubbed the Matchmaking Mamas could check two more names off their list.

If you enjoyed ***Falling For Her Best Friend***, don't miss the next book in the *Love in Holiday*

Junction series. Vi's friend, Lena, gets her chance at love with ***Falling for Her Biggest Headache.***

Download it today!

Special Thanks

My editor, Kathie Spitz

My proofreader, Amy Gamache at Rose David Editing

My formatter, Tammy Clarke at Formatting by Tammy

My awesome PA, Brittany Hively

The T.M. Franklin Book Club and T.M. Franklin ARC Team

Jamie Onderisin, Toni Wall-Thrantham, and Kathie Spitz for naming our wonderful hero, Kade.

...and of course, to my amazing family for their never ending support.

Love in Holiday Junction

Falling for Her Best Friend

Falling for Her Biggest Headache

Falling for Her Opposing Counsel

Falling for the Wrong Guy

A Fun and Quirky YA Romance

How to Get Ainsley Bishop to Fall in Love with You

A Magical Holiday Romance

Second Chances

Visions of Sugar Plums

Adventure and Romance on the High Seas

Cutlass

Short stories

A Piece of Cake

Fantasy Adventures, Written as T.M. Franklin

The MORE Trilogy

"Reminiscent of the Mortal Instruments series... only better!"
– Penny Dreadful Reviews

MORE

The Guardians

TWELVE

The New Super Humans

Super Humans

Super Powers

Super Natural

Super Heroes

Short Stories

Unscheduled Departure

Tami Franklin writes clean and wholesome romance that will sweep you away. A former TV news producer and freelance writer, she now enjoys sharing stories about people destined to be together... they just might need a little help getting there.

Franklin lives in the Pacific Northwest with her family, and a crazy dog named Bond (James Bond.)

She also writes contemporary and YA fantasy under the penname T.M. Franklin.

Find out more at www.TMFranklin.com

And to be the first notified about upcoming releases, sales, and giveaways, subscribe to Tami Franklin's mailing list especially for sweet romance at tmfranklin.com/SweetSubscriber

All new subscribers get a FREE copy of her lighthearted, opposites-attract romance, *Drive Me Crazy*!